JUST ENCASE THEY
THINK YOU'RE
STUPID

by

GEORGE C. KEEFE

www.encasement.com

Dedication

To John (Jack) and Wanda Keefe, my life blood.

Table of Contents

ILLUSTRATIONS

Front Cover Design: George C. Keefe
Back cover Design: George C. Keefe, Ian Bardsley (2 Cents Productions)
Inside Book Bottle Picture: Ian Bardsley (2 Cents Productions)

TABLES

IMPORTANT TERMS

TEM - Time, Effort/Energy/Environment, Money
MTG - Minutes To Go
VOC - Volatile Organic Content
ODS - Ozone Depleting Substances
LBP - Lead Based Paint
ACM - Asbestos Containing Materials

Acknowledgements

A special thanks to Susan Bardsley, my business partner and friend, who has shown incredible courage, persistence, and positive attitude in the face of major challenges. Without her, this book may not have been possible. Big thanks also to Bob and Ian Bardsley who comprise the spectacular Team Bardsley.

Thanks to the other people who helped with and encouraged this book:
Anita, Andrew, and Liz
Vida Chavez-Garcia
Adhiratha Keefe
Tom Keefe
Joseph P. Fearon, D.D.S.
Gerald J. Karches, M.S.
Leonard Kaye
Ed Kranepool
Scott W. Epstein, Esq.
Ron Swoboda
Niels H. Lauersen, M.D., Ph.D.
The Honorable Alan Wheat
Steve Chisholm
Anthony Corso
Cindi Sansone Braff
Mahiruha Klein
Gracelyn, Paulyn, and Apple
All my family and friends for their continued love, support, and inspiration

Introduction

Just Encase They Think You're Stupid is a brief and timely guide for everyone, from novice to professional, demystifying the sometimes complicated issues associated with hazardous materials. This simple and entertaining book offers logical and practical solutions using Green Coatings to in-place manage asbestos and lead-based paint.

A Day in a Life

"If one life makes a difference, then one day in a life can affect many."

"If possibilities could be set by facts and the moral choices one makes for the good of all, this will be the day that one makes a difference..."

New Idea

"A new idea is first condemned as ridiculous
And then dismissed as trivial, until finally,
It becomes what everybody knows."

William James

TIME Tick Tock

E
N
V
I
R
O
N
M
E
N
T

Whoosshh

Money

$ Cha Ching

My life is my message.
- Mahatma Gandhi

Life's unfairness is not irrevocable;
we can help balance the scales for others,
if not always for ourselves.
- Hubert Humphrey

The be-all and end-all of life
should not be to get rich,
but to enrich the world.
- B.C. Forbes

The meaning of life is to help others,
what other meaning could there be.
- Albert Einstein

CHAPTER 1

"The Day"

Smoke from a building fire, raging on the next block, drifted by the open windows. Sirens blared in the background as two Washington D.C. uniformed police officers informed the chief of a bomb threat, three buildings down. They told him it wasn't necessary to evacuate the building yet, but he could, if he was so inclined. There wasn't a chance of that happening, as this was Chief's last day in public service, a day that would imminently affect so many lives.

As if the fire and bomb threat weren't enough, Chief had gotten word that a small plane had accidentally flown into restrictive airspace over the White House and that the city was on high alert.

Tick Tock ... 8:30 AM and tensions were already running high. The added police presence was making people anxious. Withholding information from them would undoubtedly lead from uneasiness to panic, potentially vacating the hearing hall. As the police left, Chief calmly faced the confounded crowd and began to give them the information at hand.

He stated in a low, reassuring voice, "The disturbance down the street is nothing for all of you to worry about, and everything is under control. The hearing will start on time, promptly at 9 AM, and in the meantime, there is coffee and donuts at the back of the room, so please help yourself."

Chief's explanation seemed to calm everyone, yet amongst the distress he saw an expression of satisfaction. Dracoff was grinning, as he certainly had the most to gain from the confusion.

Chief and his panel had developed a thorough strategy of putting Dracoff in his place. As Chief looked out the window, he was slightly alarmed at the sight of the quickly falling snow, now thickening into white stacks. Whoosh...

It was questionable, now, as to whether Chief's troops would arrive on time. Tick Tock...

The windows in this soon to be demolished historic and antiquated building had to be left open. Although the heating worked, it was only at one temperature: unbearably high. As this was the last hearing and the building's final day of use, nobody thought it was worth fixing. They decided

1

that leaving the windows open would balance things out. Unfortunately, the smoke and noise that filtered in added to the room's already confusing atmosphere.

Chief and his staff had to pick the most competent individuals from a list of three hundred predominantly exceptional people to testify. Because they were the best in their field, it was a certainty that they would be "well-versed" in the pros and cons of asbestos and lead-based paint issues. Some were members of Mensa and other such brainiack communities, much like those with which Chief associated. That said Chief was keenly aware that possessing a high IQ didn't automatically make someone a competent thinker.

Chief was often amazed and amused when working with intellectual groups that were so good at identifying and categorizing a problem yet stumped at coming up with a simple solution. Oftentimes, the answer was delivered by someone who was not scholarly or academic, just the average Joe.

The priority of the day was to gather all the facts and solutions to the issues concerning environmentally hazardous materials, especially asbestos and lead-based paint. Only three options would be presented. The first was full blown removal; the second was to ignore the situation at hand and do nothing; and last to "in-place-manage" such materials.

———

CHAPTER 2

Chief

Affectionately known by co-workers, family, and friends as "Chief," the nickname stuck after he became Chief Steward in the Merchant Marines. Although proud of his accomplishment, it was his shipmates who insisted that he get the name "Chief" tattooed on his arm, while on leave.

Tick Tock ... Forty years later, although the tattoo had blurred away into his black skin, the nickname held strong. Chief was tall, slender, and looked like a cross between Morgan Freeman and Nelson Mandela, and he had the resolve of both.

Being black shaped his worldviews on several issues, especially his feelings on asbestos and lead exposure, particularly when it came to who was being unnecessarily exposed and why. Chief knew that money was needlessly expended on removal and replacement when those funds could be better spent on improving people's lives and their environments, doing more with less.

Chief, making sure he would be well rested for one of the most important days of his life, had gone to bed earlier than usual the night before. Chief didn't like going to bed any earlier than he was accustomed, due to the logical fact that it cut away from the 1,440 minutes offered in a day. Nevertheless, he also found logic and comfort in that he would be cutting into the 1440 minutes of this day, rather than tomorrow: The Day.

Chief lost his wife several years ago. As a widower, he mostly focused on his work, making sure it always had meaning. Now single and living a simple, frugal life, he was very content to be surrounded by clocks, caring for only himself, his books, and a lone houseplant.

As a youngster, he had begun counting the minutes wasting away, day by day. Within his mind was a consistent, tick tock of time. At first, he viewed the days as grains of sand in an hourglass, always slipping away. This view, however, made him anxious, and he recognized the elements of counter-productivity in such negativity. As a result, he began to count the remaining minutes left in a day or the time left to accomplish a task. He referred to this as MTG (Minutes To Go), and it aided in driving him optimistically forward, continuously advancing. His co-workers were familiar with his coined term, MTG, and so it was commonly used.

When Chief stated "15-MTG," all knew that there were fifteen minutes to go. When one of his team said MTG, he found himself not only computing MTG in a task but also the MTG in a day. The only time he looked back was purely for the sake of reflection on the productivity of tasks and how things could be done better and faster in the future.

At one point, he even started counting heartbeats in an hour, then in a day. He calculated the average beats per hour and compared them, simultaneously, to his calculations of MTG in each daily task. Although consuming and comforting both at the same time, he found this inaccurate, due to the difference in variations of heartbeats per hour and per day.

One such factor revealed itself to him when in the presence of Lyn, with whom he was infatuated, causing his heartbeat to skip irregularly. Because of this, he stuck to minutes, a true constant. After another experiment in which he had begun calculating seconds per day, he had quickly realized the counter-productivity in such a task and concluded to stick to rounding off to the closest minute.

Chief was big on to-do lists. He would prioritize six of the most important things to do the following day. He would put each list together the night before and assign the minutes he would spend on each task. Some tasks would take longer than others, and the allotted time estimation per task were always amazingly accurate. This precise regimen became an art form, his flow, his direction, and with it, each day ran more smoothly than the last. The more he practiced it, the more accurate he became. Throughout his life, he had come to find comfort in the presence of clocks. At home and in his office, he surrounded himself with clocks and therefore was always privy to instantaneously calculating the minutes he had to work with, the MTG. Tick Tock…

With what most saw as an obsession, Chief was able to calculate the MTG at any time during the day. For example, he only slept six hours a night (360 min.), from 11:00 PM to 5:00 AM, giving him a total of 1080 minutes to work with for that day. He knew how much time he needed to shave (3 min.), shower (7 min.), eat breakfast (11 min.), drive to work and park his car (23 min.), and finally, to walk to his desk (3 min.). All of this was done in 47 minutes, which not only gave him a nice, round prime number but also left him with 1,033 MTG.

Due to his near resentment of having to stop for nourishment, seeing the whole process as inefficient (considering it simply as fuel for the body), he often avoided the chore. In his perspective, the task was a simple and obvious waste of minutes. The plain act of chewing wasted motion and threatened the maximizing of his minutes. Lunch was always a protein shake, sucked back during work or while reading.

Earlier in life, Chief was influenced about time and not wasting it when he found out that one of his family members had a terminal illness and was given a short time to live. After that, he always respected his minutes and forever tried to maximize them.

He chose to be a vegetarian, seeing it as the most economic body fuel. In truth, it was the most efficient use of the planet's resources and the least stressful on the earth.

It also took less chomps before swallowing, saving time and motion.

He was consumed with value engineering and always geared his very existence to get more done in less time, effort/energy/environment, and money: TEM (Time, Effort/Energy/Environment, Money). Because of this mindset, he stuck to minutes; to Chief, they were the only true constant. With dependable time established as a constant, his next priority was set on effort, energy and environmental concerns. Whoosh ... and then the money...Cha-Ching.

Chief was identified early on as a natural talent with exceptional creative ability, a genius, someone highly skilled. He had an unusual mental ability, exceptional intellectual power, and true originality.

In his youth, he won the Westinghouse award at eleven years old. He was published at eighteen, received two doctorates, one from MIT in Civil Engineering and the other from Harvard in Organization and Management. After completing his PhDs, he taught at Princeton for two years before being diagnosed with OCD (Obsessive Compulsive Disorder).

He knew full well what he had and that others may view it as a disorder, but he never considered it to be such in any way for himself. More so, Chief perceived this so-called "disorder" as a gift. His obsessive and compulsive behavior was a magnificent personality quirk, one that benefited rather than handicapped him. He was a fan of numbers and counting. Chief loved prime numbers because, after all, the odds were in favor of prime numbers. His favorite prime number was the number 3, as in the Holy Trinity, the Three Musketeers, the Three Stooges, "Three times a lady," Three's

Company, "Three strikes and you're out," the Three-peat, three branches of government, three parts of a day (480 minutes each, morning, noon, and night), three meals a day (breakfast, lunch, and dinner), and today, his team would consist of three members. Obsessive Compulsive Disorder was certainly a gift, and he was in no way hindered by it. Most people never saw Chief's OCD; to them, he was a guy with extraordinary talents, always accomplishing his goals by hitting his budgetary and time targets.

From youth, he counted everything and anything, from the cracks in the sidewalk to the number of cars on the trains that sped by. Numbers were never simply just numbers to him. They were always TEM numbers, time, Tick Tock; an element of the environment, Whoosh; plus money, Cha-Ching. They were all, in effect, related to one another through MTG.

As an adult he had his OCD under control by no longer counting things like cracks in a sidewalk or the cars on a passing train. He never counted anything that didn't produce positive results. Numbers, time and dollars, coincided with his priorities. Later in life, he began focusing on the environment as well.

It was exactly the perspective and priorities that Chief mastered that made him so good at construction projects, overseeing them and knowing precisely where to apply the value engineering. He could quickly add up all the factors within a job and instantly calculate the most effective course of action. With his expert ability to count time and estimate costs, he knew that 9 times out of 10, when dealing with solid hazardous materials, in-place-management was certainly the best and the most cost effective way to go. Chief had compiled tons of facts and figures over the years verifying this, although today he would let outside experts confirm the facts.

Within minutes of stepping onto a jobsite, he would assess the project and conclude the most effective plan of action. In evaluating a problem or situation, even a person, Chief was quick and accurate. With a person, he would throw out a short metaphor, a quick cliché, or a one-line joke. Receiving an answer or even just a look would tell him what he needed to know about an individual: if that person's strength was right or left brained, if they had a sense of humor, and how that person may be a help or be a hindrance.

His mind worked faster than most and yet he was patient with others who needed to mull things over, although for him this process was a waste of time. He was able to identify and eliminate those who had analyses paralysis, that kept taking a situation apart yet frozen from coming up with a solution.

His years were finally catching up with him, and he knew retirement was close at hand. Before his imminent swan song, he was determined to make a positive change in the world for people and their environment. Today, he would do just that.

His extensive research and experience had reinforced in his mind the unmistakable superiority of in-place asbestos and lead-based paint management. After all, he did have ample, basic commonsense on his side. However, sometimes he found that commonsense wasn't as common as it once was.

Chief was an expert at using Kipling's six, honest serving men. Their names were Who, What, When, Where, How and Why. He refused to make a decision without them, as it was these honest folk, and the Ben Franklin balance sheet, that he relied on to help him make all his important decisions. Chief never came to a conclusion or a determination without being armed with such reliable, trustworthy, and logical ammunition.

Looking around the room, on the verge of disarray, only strengthened the Chief's determination to remain in control. At this point, the only one in the room smiling was...Dracoff

———

CHAPTER 3

Dracoff

Dracoff Joseph Procrusties was otherwise known as "Dracoff the Misguided." Chief had heard many refer to him as such, and worse. Dracoff stood to gain the most from the chaos that was about to ensue. Chief liked most people and got along with just about everyone. He believed that sometimes he needed to do business with people for whom he didn't care and understood the very basic principle that, like a politician, if he only wanted the people he liked to vote for him, he'd never be elected.

Chief knew that Dracoff had harmful, greedy intentions, making him difficult to like and hard to deal with. Yet he also knew a little about his past and upbringing, sympathizing with him and the circumstances that made him into who he was. One of Chief's assistants jokingly said that Dracoff needed a trip to the vet to be neutered, so there would never be an offspring.

Chief was sure that Dracoff gave this feeling to many, but being a professional, he never spoke negatively about him. Dracoff was smug, only because he didn't have a clue what Chief had in store for him.

Dracoff was a master of deception, who had keen insights into human nature. He had been called "Phony Dough Joe," due to his middle name being Joseph, and his involvement in laundering money through a local bakery. This certainly topped his long list of other felonies and convictions.

Even today, it would not be found beyond his character to forge insurance documents or falsify the testing of products, using the old bait and switch method of substituting materials. Using this tactic, the results and approvals of another company or materials were specified. If he didn't forge a document with blatant gall, he would use deceptive wording or phrasing like "complies with," "conforms to," or adheres to," so the unsuspecting client would believe they were getting one thing, only to be supplied with an inferior imitation. He had, in the past, made unsubstantiated claims, gambling on the truth of his products or statements not being revealed. He was a man without shame.

Dracoff was short, pudgy, and balding. He had beady, sunken eyes, surrounded by dark rings, resembling (in the utmost uncanny fashion) the polluted ozone layer around the planet. He always dressed in cheap, frumpy suits and used pungent colognes, which he only assumed masked his unhygienic stench. The mere sight of him was enough to frighten small children and adults alike. Often, folks would comment that, somewhere, a bridge was missing its troll.

Despite his appearance and unpleasant personal hygiene, Dracoff was very intelligent, and yet, he never used his intelligence for the betterment of anything or anyone other than himself. It appeared that if a situation presented a break-even outcome, he found it a pure loss rather than a gain, despite the situations of the others involved. He only used his intelligence for profit and always looked for the opportunity to take advantage of the weak and less fortunate, regardless of just how much the benefits favored him. He simply seemed to enjoy being wicked, getting the upper hand. Sometimes, he did so only because he could, with no monetary gain, only a depraved, personal reward. He seemed to derive pleasure from others' suffering, revealing his morally objectionable behavior.

Rarely was Dracoff stupid enough to challenge someone of equal or greater power. He would always lie in wait, lurking for bad situations to arise, and then make his move, swooping in to take advantage. Much akin to a vulture awaiting an unaware animal to fall sickly, he would make his attacks. Dracoff was undoubtedly similar to a sneaky Gollum-like creature, constantly skulking in the background; waiting to take advantage of any he may consider easy prey. Today, he was no different.

A lot of Dracoff's unhappy personality was the product of his upbringing. Deserted by his single mother at three years old, he was shifted between orphanages and foster homes. Because of necessity, these places taught frugalness, which Dracoff misinterpreted as getting as much as you can, disregarding how that was accomplished or at whomever's expense. The one redeeming act of generosity Dracoff exemplified was in making contributions to some of the orphanages through which he had passed.

Dracoff sat in the back of the discussion hall with his eyes cunningly sizing each and every person in the room, his aura unsettling the entire crowd surrounding him.

Chief had a well thought out strategy of putting Dracoff in his place. He had assembled a team to counter Dracoff's group. However, as Chief looked out the window at the snow piling up outside, his troops arriving on time was starting to look questionable. Whoosh.

There had been many significantly memorable days in Chief's life: the day his father moved the family out of the projects, the day he graduated from college and received his PhDs, accomplishing the world class feat of swimming the English Channel, the day he married his wife, the day his daughter was born, and each day of promotion during his career. All played such memorable parts in his life.

Yet this day, at the Washington D.C. City Council Public Hearing, was indeed one of the most significant of days. This day was one in which the issues concerning asbestos and lead-based paint would be discussed in front of many, and due to the outcome, the impact would affect the lives of many, making it the most important of all days for Chief.

This was a hearing with some media attention, so much so that some international governments were sending a delegation to "observe the deliberation of building hazards" on their country's behalf. Chief was aware that many countries worldwide had asbestos and lead-based paint problems, primarily due to the lack of education, management, and regulations on these potential hazards. Sadly, even when these things were in place, if there was no enforcement, there were those who would cheat and unnecessarily expose many to such hazards. It was apparent that the issues concerning lead-based paint were not only still beginning to be identified, but both asbestos and lead-based paint were still in constant use.

The goal of the day was to give the novice, the professional, and everyone in between a brief education on the Who, What, Where, When, Why and How of asbestos and lead-based paint. The conclusion was to address logical, practical solutions.

Chief had done the hours of research and had gathered years of information involving asbestos and lead-based paint, from all available channels, completely covering the logical methods of dealing with such potential hazardous materials.

When asked to put together a solutions panel to testify on these hazards, it didn't take Chief long to decide to whom he would entrust this invaluable work. His group would present the facts on asbestos and lead-based paint and then elaborate on the safest, most cost-effective manner of eliminating exposure. The panel's conclusion had to be a clear-cut agreement, if environmental security was at all a priority.

He had networked himself with a number of experts, for he believed knowledge was more important than material passions or possessions.

He was fascinated with brainpower and valued it above all else. He knew that intelligence wasn't just IQ; it included emotional intelligence, cognitive reasoning, and basic common sense. He conferred with consultants, industrial hygienists, physicists, engineers, architects, lawyers, insurance agents, teachers, contractors; and his favorite were housewives, who also seemed to use Kipling's six, honest serving men instinctively, asking lots of questions. All were of the best at what they did, and Chief was relying on them.

Some of these professionals believed that there was a clear conspiracy to cover up and withhold important information, or even worse, a deliberate intention to provide the wrong information in order to greatly benefit the few at the tragic expense of the many. Cha-ching. Otis was one of the dedicated believers in such a conspiracy.

———

CHAPTER 4

Otis

Dr. Otis Ben Israel, AKA Otis the Passionate had a PhD in Organization and Management, and while his credentials allowed him a cushy office job, he was never one to take advantage of his position. He loved the field and the camaraderie of the jobsite. He was truly in his element when working with people to accomplish tangible goals. Suit sporting, paper pushing, and desk jockeying was certainly nothing anyone could accuse Otis of doing. Chief, however, insisted that he wear a suit when delivering his testimony. There was no doubt in Otis's mind that the uncomfortable monkey attire would have him completely soaked in his own sweat within a short time, yet he knew that Chief was right.

Otis was a short, stocky man, often nervous, and frequently sweaty. These characteristics were well exaggerated when public speaking was on his agenda. He never wore any sort of accessories: rings, watches, or any other type of jewelry. He was, however, a yarmulke-wearing, barrel-chested, bull of a man, with a heart of gold. He always strived to do the right thing and consistently leaned toward the defense of the underdog. Along with protecting people, he always had the well being of the planet in mind with whatever action he took. He had an extensive background in coatings and was expertly cross-trained in the removal and in-place-management of asbestos, lead-based paint, and other hazardous materials. Otis was also very well versed with regard to the most cost effective system designs and applications of quality green, renewable, and sustainable coatings.

Otis first got involved with hazardous materials when a close friend who was an asbestos removal contractor told him of attending an asbestos removal pre-bid job-walk through a school in one of the poorer areas of town. The job was for the complete removal and replacement of spray on asbestos fireproofing on structural steel.

The thing that struck Otis's friend as odd was that this asbestos was in perfect shape, and when air monitoring was done, it showed that there was no fiber release or any contamination. When this contractor asked why they were removing and replacing it, the answer was "Because it's there." This was completely crazy, seeing that there weren't enough books or desks for the kids, and the teachers' salaries were horrible, yet they were going to spend what amounted to over a million dollars to remove and replace asbestos that was in good shape. When Otis heard this, he knew there was a better way: to simply cover it up.

Otis was a modest owner of one of the largest and most profitable coating companies in the country, focusing on everything from bridge and dam work, right down to custom and fine finishes. Otis attributed his success, always, to doing what was best for the client—no matter the possibility of profit losses in the short term. He believed that the difference between the companies that thrived and those that didn't was solely based on the quality of products used and customer service. Otis's motto around the work place was: "When you take care of the customer, in the end, the customer will take care of you."

Otis always had an attitude of gratitude for all he had in life and felt sorry for people when he would hear them complain about their jobs, hating Mondays, and looking forward to Fridays and the weekend. He never understood why they didn't pick something they could have a passion for, enjoying and taking pride in their jobs. He believed in and always shared Confucius' saying: "Pick a job you love, and you will never have to work a day in your life."

Otis felt so fortunate that he found his niche early in life. He wasn't sure why and never questioned it. He just knew he loved coating things. It made him uncomfortable to see structures wearing away that could be shielded with a coating. He was never at ease seeing unprotected, naked buildings.

Chief's most memorable experience with Otis was during a pre-bid job-walk. Otis got into an argument with a fellow bidder on the quality of materials that should be used. The competing bidder had stated that he did not want to use products that had an extensive life-span. His inconsiderate contention had been that the use of a second or third-rate cheap material would ensure future job prospects for him or fellow painters, within a few years. Otis was quick to point out that this theory of planned obsolescence was a selfish way to handle a project and that although the silent thought of such a scheme was one thing, to state such blasphemy in the Chief's presence was an act of pure stupidity. It was from that point on that the Chief valued Otis' opinions. When putting together his panel, he knew that Otis, with all his passion and commitment to excellence, would surely create a bold defense, and therefore, he was assigned to the solutions panel.

Otis was a strong advocate for in-place management, the covering up of potentially hazardous materials with quality green, renewable, and sustainable coatings. He saw the obvious bang for the buck, compared to all the downsides of unnecessary removal and replacement.

The only reservation Chief had about Otis was that he had a tendency to speak his mind, sometimes out of turn, and never did he worry about those he offended, especially if those with hurt feelings had an ill-intended agenda.

Chief was confident in that Otis would get the facts out there and that he would make sure that everyone in the room would be made privy to the benefits of management in-place with green coatings, along with the notion that, most often, it was the only logical way of handling asbestos and lead-based paint. The problem was that a lot of people had a challenge registering the most simple and obvious. As the saying goes, "You can lead a horse to water, but you can't make him drink." With Otis assigned to act as a reference guide, Chief now needed an exceptional speaker, someone to present and simplify the details and jargon. The Chief's extensive network consisted of many who could accomplish this, but only one was capable of doing it with finesse.

———

CHAPTER 5

Marcos

Dr. Marcos Grey, AKA Marcos the Smooth was always dressed impeccably in dark grey or dark blue double-breasted suits, with white shirts, silk ties, black socks, and spit-shine wing-tipped shoes. At six feet four inches and with his dark complexion, he may have been one of the most handsome men in the world. His comforting, easy-going personality instantly put everyone at ease, especially in the most stressing of circumstances. To Chief, Marcos was a no-brainer candidate for his panel. His information was always right on; he never guessed at anything, as he was a stickler for conducting proper research before jumping into any situation, as in Sun Tzu's *The Art of War*. This ensured the battle was won, long before it had begun.

Marcos received his LLB with distinction from Harvard University and went on to receive his PhD in Comparative Sociology/Historical Sociology & Quantitative Methodology from Harvard Gradate School. He was also a Wharton graduate, with distinction, as well as a large real estate developer and author of several *NY Times* best-sellers.

He was an independently wealthy entrepreneur and lived off of his real-estate investments, which gave much more depth to his occupation, never basing his decisions on a paycheck. Like Otis, he firmly stood by the righteous underdog.

Marcos had an inquisitive way of assessing any situation and always answered business questions with one defining question in return, "What is best for the consumer and the environment?" He didn't look solely at the financial implications of this question but the health and safety issues as well. The short and long-term environmental aspects of each decision were weighed accordingly.

Marcos was sometimes accused of being cold and calculating; some claimed that he only saw things in black and white. He would refute matter-of-factly that he did not see in black nor white but in black and red, right and wrong, and just and unjust. It seemed as though he always had the right answers, due to his ability to quickly come to his conclusions. In addition, he always made the most of his decisions, based on what was called the Ben Franklin Balance Sheet, which he had learned from Chief.

Ben Franklin, a great forefather of the United States, always made his most important decisions by taking a sheet of paper and drawing a line down the center. On this sheet, he would list the pros on one side and the cons on the other. He would then weigh them in contrast and base his decisions depending on which side carried the most logic.

Marcos took to this process in the most extreme fashion. His balance sheet consisted not only of the simple pros and cons but also of the extensive pros and cons of said individual items listed. For instance, even with a seemingly simple question asked of people every day while grocery shopping, "Would you like paper or plastic?" Marcos had taken the simple question and analyzed the pros and cons far beyond the obvious (what was the most convenient, what was easiest to carry, what took up less space to store, which was easiest to throw away, which had the least impact on the environment, and which contained potential leaking items). Rather, Marcos had created a balance sheet in which the TEM was the primary focus, the effect of paper and plastic on the environment, over a period of time and at what costs.

He would ask the question with TEM in mind, and only when both sides had been properly weighed would he conclude with an answer. There were times, however, when a clear-cut, black and white answer would not be available to him, and only a middle-ground solution, one in which the TEM would play a part (i.e. recycling the bags, always taking them back to the store for reuse, or using another renewable reusable item like a canvas bag), would seem the only proper action.

Marcos always looked for unexplored options. Such was the case when the only solutions that were presented for dealing with asbestos or lead-based paint were to leave it alone or fully remove it. He found and presented a third option.

If Marcos was asked if he thought it was better for the average consumer to use oil or gas heating, out would come the balance sheet and it would look something like this.

Oil	Gas
Non-renewable Expensive Toxic Exhaust Requires delivery (inconvenient) Only used for heating	Renewable More stable cost Cleaner burn Pipe line (convenient) Multiple household Uses
Results: The benefits of gas heating outweighed the benefits of oil heating.	

With Marcos the Smooth in his corner, Chief knew that all possible avenues of asbestos and lead-based paint would undoubtedly be covered. It would certainly be as plain as day to one and all that, on a global scale, in-place management was the best way of dealing with these hazards. Nonetheless, a dire element was still missing from the most powerful of panels.

———

CHAPTER 6

Lyn

Chief had met Dr. Lyn Lee, AKA Lyn the Caring, twenty years prior. She had been the head of the occupational therapy department for the Board of Education, and Chief distinctly remembered being entirely impressed with her knowledge on important issues and her compassion for the less fortunate. She was a wonderful blend of smarts and heart, and most certainly a perfect addition to a stunning panel.

Dr. Lyn Lee was an Occupational Therapist and had her PhD in Social Concerns. She was of the Asian descent; her Father was Taiwanese and her mother was from an island off mainland Japan called Okinawa. Lyn Lee was raised on Okinawa and attended U.S. military based schools. Her father was employed as a school administrator for the American military school system, DoDDS (Department of Defense Dependent Schools). Her mother was employed as a nurse.

Lyn had always been an exceptional individual. At the age of sixteen, she had completed the 10th grade and was intent on the career she had already chosen for herself. Lyn decided she would dedicate her time and efforts to helping others, most importantly the less fortunate. She had announced to her parents that she would be skipping the last two years of high school in order to directly attend college.

She made her way to the United States and committed herself to becoming an OT (Occupational Therapist) in New York City. Lyn graduated three years later with a Masters and the highest of honors, receiving five awards and being the valedictorian of her class. It was pretty much the same attaining her PhD. Soon afterward, she was married to her college sweetheart, and life seemed picture perfect.

Years later, Lyn found herself widowed. Her husband, only in his late thirties, had been a victim of asbestos poisoning. He developed mesothelioma and passed away, tragically. As a child, he had suffered secondary exposure to large amounts of asbestos that had been transferred to him via the clothes of his father, an Indian ship breaker.

She, much like Otis and Marcos was independently wealthy, due to several real estate investments. She now traveled around the globe, although she preferred to drive around the North American continent in her airstream trailer. The primary purpose of her travels was to gather as many facts as possible concerning the exposure and effects of lead-based paints and asbestos and then present solutions.

Lyn also dedicated her time to educating people on the proper prevention to the exposure of the hazardous poisons. She worked mostly in destitute neighborhoods and had become one of the leading experts on asbestos, lead-based paint, and its far reaching effects in the years following exposure. Like Otis, she was also an outspoken proponent of management-in-place. She targeted her seminars on the role this process would play in the solution to many of the concerns associated with asbestos, lead-based paint, and other hazardous materials.

Lyn made disagreeing without being disagreeable an art form. She had such a disarming, tender way about her. She displayed a compassionate warmth and understanding that calmed even the most abrasive disagreeable personalities. When she knew she was right, she employed a winning technique of always listening to whomever and waiting until they finished saying whatever they needed to say, no matter how long that took. Then, she would gently start to lead them to her conclusions by posing a series of questions. She knew how to guide people with great sensitivity, eventually lulling them over to her side.

Lyn was breathtaking. Standing only four feet eleven and weighing 105 pounds "wet," she was the perfect example of the phrase, "It's not the size of the dog in the fight but the size of the fight in the dog." She lived to side with the underdog, as it supplied her with a sense of true purpose. She believed in the universal purpose to aid humankind, that the happiness of one depended on the welfare of all, that those unknown to us play an important role in our personal destinies, and that we are all bound by the ties of humanity. In her eyes, class distinctions were contrary to justice, and every person deserved to be respected as an individual, with none favored or idolized. She believed that everyone should be treated as a king or queen in a kingdom where nobody wore a crown.

Chief was somewhat smitten with Lyn from the start, as was she with him. When they had initially met, however, both were happily married; therefore, neither pursued each other with anything other than a professional interest. Chief knew that her personality and experience made her a very credible individual and an excellent expert witness for his solution panel.

He was able to track her down at a conference in New Orleans, where she was the keynote speaker. She agreed to come and help in any way she could and would set her schedule accordingly.

There was no question that Lyn would be Chief's most influential and impressive member. Nobody could match Lyn's ability to intellectually and passionately convey the unnecessary suffering of those exposed to asbestos and lead-based paint, while also presenting a simple solution.

Chief knew how to efficiently manage a deliberation and the representation of panels. He also knew that he would be dealing with some people who couldn't care less about the harmful effects of asbestos and lead-based paint, especially on those who they considered inferior: of "lower" race and class. Their only concern was the impact on their wallet. Most importantly, Chief was aware that they would be trying to convert conventional wisdom, which was ignorant because all the facts were rarely brought to light.

Chief and the members of his team were involved with several worthy organizations, such as UNICEF, Habitat for Humanity, World Hunger Organization, and the Special Olympics. And as fate would have it, they were to be once more united in yet another worthy cause on this day. The stage was set for the education of all attending.

The Day would start exactly at 0900 hours and end exactly at 1800 hours, not a minute earlier or a minute later. Tick Tock. Chief had made sure that there would be no room for errors. It would be documented in text, audio, and video, which would then be translated into twenty-seven different languages, duplicated and distributed throughout the United Nations. Any interested parties, wherever in the world, could easily obtain a copy.

480 minutes worth of testimony focused primarily on the facts and the minute details Chief was determined to have brought to light. There would be panels presenting from 0900 to 1200 hours on asbestos, three panels presenting on lead-based paints from 1300 to 1600 hours, and two panels presenting on solutions from 1600 to 1800 hours. Each panel would be allowed a maximum of three panelists and would have exactly sixty minutes to present their data in one of two ways: either one person from a panel could speak for the entire time or they could divide the time among panel members as the panel saw fit.

Time is unforgiving, and so was Chief. The panels could use less than their allotted sixty minutes (which would be seen as wasteful in Chief's eyes), but would not be allotted a second more. To make sure of this, Chief had each table set up with three chairs, each equipped with microphones and a light. He had assigned one of his assistants to control both the lights and microphones and another assistant to direct people to and from the tables. So when one panel was speaking, the other would be preparing their presentations. There would be a one-minute warning tone, alerting the panel or speaker that their time was almost up, and at exactly sixty minutes, the light and microphones would go off at one table and on at the next. The next panel would start their presentation the instant the light went on.

This was a sure fire way of keeping things on track and not allowing anyone any more time than that which was allotted. There wasn't any room for the cutting into another's time or wasting any precious minutes. The stricter the time constraints, the more accurate and factual the information would be. Knowing this, the presenters would deliver more facts than opinions on the subject matter, and this way, better decisions would be made based on their testimonies.

As much as Chief knew about the topics of asbestos, lead-based paint, and the exposure to them, he was still excited to hear what new information may be presented by some of the experts.

Over the years, Chief had listened to all the pontificating blowhards he could stand, and to some during the day, it wouldn't be any different. It was enlightening, however, when there was a break from all the hogwash and lucid, helpful information was presented.

Also there were some presenting who would stand out in the crowd as heroes of the day, such as Shane Blade, the NYC firefighter who had lost so many friends during the 9/11 tragedy. He did not hesitate to go into an environmental nightmare to save whomever he could. Due to his heroism, he was now suffering the effects of exposure to the hazardous materials. There were others who stood out just for being the odd characters they were, such as Sister Mary Grace, with her yard stick delivery, who came across as firm even when she followed up her staunch statements with a caring twinkle in her eye and an affectionate smile.

All aspects of asbestos and lead-based paint would be explored from the historical, practical, industrial, and medical; including the extensive and varied uses of hazardous materials, the medical research on who is most affected by them, where these materials end up, and logical conclusions. Some present would only hear the "blah, blah, blah," negative effects, "yadee, yadee, yadee," there needs to be something done, all the while tolerantly waiting for the solutions.

Chief and many other attendees were interested in the practical solutions. The only real solutions were those comprised of the best TEM. Chief knew it was up to his panel to explain these valuable and timely conclusions in the simplest terms possible. What it came down to was a duel of factual information against sometimes deliberate misinformation, cover-ups, and lies of omission.

What Dracoff never understood and never would was that Chief didn't consider it as any type of conflict. To him, it was just negative misinformation up against the positive flow of correct education. What mattered was how it was presented and that it was easily understood. Chief knew that whatever deceptive information Dracoff may have up his sleeve, it would be countered with accurate information.

To Chief, it was "all good."

Chief looked from his watch to the table that had been set up for Panel One and counted down the seconds before the table's signal was to be turned on. Panel One was composed of an historian, a scientist, and a researcher, all of whom had backgrounds investigating asbestos in their areas of expertise ... 15, 14, 13. Tick Tock.

It was their job to present unbiased facts about asbestos, and while the Chief had already done his homework, it was important to have other experts get the facts out... 10, 9, 8. Tick ... "Urban planners, developers, and government officials had taken false information as true and accurate for far too long, with devastating consequences for the men, women, and children from poor neighborhoods, with minority backgrounds." Tock.

Chief looked to the table ... 3, 2, 1. The lights flickered on, and the first asbestos panelist began. Chief smiled briefly, as the efficiency of The Day had been initiated beautifully.

———

CHAPTER 7

Asbestos

The first panelist started with the naturally occurring mineral known as "quicklime" in Latin and "asbestos" in Greek, and how it had been used throughout history.

> The Ancient Greeks began using asbestos some two thousand years ago, weaving it into the clothing of slaves. After realizing its flame-resistant properties they coined its name, "asbestos."
>
> The Ancient Romans, like the Greeks, used asbestos for its insulation and flame-retardant properties.

Chief would see slight interest in the crowd when certain facts were brought up, like how asbestos tablecloths and napkins could be found in many restaurants because of their flame retardant capabilities.

> They could be thrown into the fire to remove food and other debris and then placed back on the table in time enough for the next customer. The Romans named asbestos "amanitas," meaning "unpolluted," because after being in the fire, the cloth would come out whiter than it went in.
>
> Marco Polo documented cases of being shown asbestos items, such as asbestos cloth on his travels.

Most of this testimony was bland, and yet there were some interesting facts that even Chief didn't know. For instance, during medieval times, the panelist had explained,

> Because some forms of asbestos resemble old wood, asbestos crosses would be carved and sold as "wooden"

crosses that were carved directly from the "true cross," on which Jesus Christ was crucified. These conscienceless merchants would show the validity of their "divine products" by showing how the crosses could withstand fire without burning.

Early identification of the harmful effects was brought up. For example, the harmful biological effects of asbestos were first recognized by the Greek geographer, Strabo, who noticed many slaves who wore the asbestos cloth began to suffer from sickness of the lungs. Caius Plinius Secundus (23 AD – August 24, 79 AD), better known as Pliny the Elder, was an ancient author, naturalist, philosopher, naval and military commander, and author of *Naturalis Historia*. He is known for his saying, "True glory consists in doing what deserves to be written, in writing what deserves to be read." He also noted the adverse effects of asbestos and observed that people who were exposed to large amounts of asbestos for long periods of time were more prone to "lung sickness," especially those who worked in the asbestos mines. He suggested the use of a respirator made of transparent bladder skin to protect workers from asbestos dust.

The decline of asbestos didn't occur until it was undeniably identified as a health hazard in the 1970s, after which it was banned in the United States and some other developed countries. The last major asbestos mines closed in Australia in 1983, and while most asbestos types have not been exported since 1984, chrysotile (white asbestos) is still being imported until new asbestos regulations come into effect.

Most asbestos fibers are not visible to the naked eye, and there are no immediate symptoms of exposure such as coughing, sneezing, or itching. Therefore, you cannot tell if asbestos is in the air, if you are being exposed, or even if you have inhaled it without proper air monitoring.

To regulate asbestos exposure OSHA, the Occupational Safety and Health Administration, has set the fiber limit. The EPA has proposed that the acceptable concentration limits of asbestos in drinking water are 7 million fibers per liter of long fibers, at lengths greater than or equal to 5 μm. It's also been stated that there is no safe exposure limit.

Breaking down and disintegrating, asbestos becomes airborne and suspended in air like dust and breathable. Most breathable asbestos fibers are not visible to the unaided human eye and range in sizes from about 3.0-20.0 μm in length to as thin as 0.01 μm. To give you a point of reference, human hair ranges in size from 17 to 181 μm. As the fibers get smaller and lighter, they become more easily airborne and introducible to the body's respiratory system. The fibers will eventually settle like most house dust but are easily re-suspended in air by air currents or other forms of disturbance.

Over the last century, it is estimated that over 30 million tons of asbestos have been used in the United States alone. Approximately three thousand products have been produced that use asbestos in some form or other. It has been used extensively as a building material both in new and refurbished construction, and was widely used in surface-applied finishes for acoustical, decorative, and fire-retardant applications. Many manufactured goods benefited from asbestos, including: roofing, ceiling tiles, flooring materials, all types of coatings, thermal insulation, and texturing materials.

Even though it was banned in 1974 in the USA, this did not mean it wasn't used. Packing plants, storage facilities, and contractors still had great deals of the banned asbestos-containing materials, and they were not going to absorb the losses due to new regulation. They would ship and use these materials a little at a time. As a result, buildings constructed after 1974 still test positive for asbestos.

The types of asbestos that are most problematic to the general public today tend to involve Spray-on fire-proofing on structural steel, pipes, HVAC ducts, and roofing materials, such as Transite.

The use of asbestos to manufacture Transite was phased out in the United States in the 1970s. However, older varieties of Transite were made of 12-50 percent asbestos and cement, leading to its frequent use for such purposes as furnace flues, roof shingles, siding, and wallboard for areas where being fire retardant materials are particularly important. It was also used in walk-in coolers made in large supermarkets in the 1960s, all the way through to the 1980s. Other uses included roof drain piping, sanitary sewer drain piping, and HVAC duct insulation.

Because cutting, breaking, and machining transite releases carcinogenic asbestos fibers into the air, its use has fallen out of favor in the USA, and yet is still produced and widely used in other countries.

Transite roofing and wall siding was available as early as 1929 and is still widely used throughout the world.

Over time, this material gets harder and more brittle, having little flexibility and no elongation.

Some of the most common materials that contained asbestos were:

Roofing and wall siding

Built up roofing

Coal tar base materials

Composition shingles

Roll roofing

Roof Mastic

Plaster

Acoustic ceilings (Popcorn ceilings)

Paints (Galbestos)

Floor tile, VAT (Vinyl Asbestos Tile)

Floor Adhesive Mastic

Also included was spray-on fireproofing, ranging

from the light fluffy cotton candy type to the hard

cementitious material.

Even though asbestos was outlawed in the United States in1974, studies have been released proving that it was still produced and used up into the late 1980s; as with vermiculite, a material containing asbestos that was used in garden products; fireproofing, cement mixtures, attic insulation and other consumer products, showing damagingly high contents of asbestos.

Testimony brought up that testing didn't always detect the asbestos content due to its tendency to not be distributed evenly. A test in one area could turn up "clean" while another test done just inches away could turn up "dirty," that is testing positive for asbestos. As well, testing results could be manipulated by those doing the analyses and it was important that companies doing the work were not the ones monitoring the results.

Dracoff wasn't smiling at this point. Chief reflected on those known incidents where Dracoff was fined and almost prosecuted for things like falsifying samples, forging documents, and not following proper safety measures. He constantly misled clients by telling them that they were at risk when they weren't and that their only option to prevent exposure was to fully remove materials. He often cut corners on his jobsites and put his workers and the general public at risk. For instance, he would have decontamination chambers with showers set up on the jobsite, but no water for the shower. He would run his clean air clearance samples back at his office, guaranteeing them to pass. He thought nothing of forging everything from insurance certificates to employee worker certifications and medical records, just to put a few more dollars in his pocket. The crazy thing was this was during the early days of asbestos removal, when doing everything by the book meant huge profits, and thus, no reason to cheat.

Chief knew that Dracoff was connected to several high profile corruption scandals, but unfortunately, it wasn't proven in court. Dracoff had more often than not slipped through the cracks, claiming ignorance. When that failed, he would find a fall guy, or worse, an innocent bystander to take the blame.

The panelist went on.

Quite often, guilty contractors are caught and cited for hiring undocumented workers who lack the necessary experience and training, or protection to legally remove asbestos. Contractors who ignore safety regulations in removing asbestos or other hazardous materials commit an environmental crime, which exposes countless people to potentially fatal and excruciatingly painful lung diseases.

The panelist also brought to light that in-place management of asbestos has now been seen as a preferred method of abatement, minimizing the need for jobsite controls and the opportunity to cheat. This was backed up in a startling reversal of existing policy.

The United States Environmental Protection Agency published in June 1990 standards for managing asbestos in buildings instead of removing the carcinogenic material. In fact, it was William Reilly, Chief EPA Administrator who said, "It is the opinion of EPA professionals that very often the best thing to do about asbestos when you find it in your building is to manage it." EPA chief Reilly also said that most asbestos removal in this country is unnecessary and that asbestos removal is inherently dangerous because it often creates more air contamination than when left alone.

More revealing facts were given.

Asbestos exposure results when asbestos fibers enter the body, most commonly, via inhalation or ingestion. Once inhaled or ingested these fibers have the potential of remaining in the lungs and intestines for a lifetime.

At times, it takes up to fifteen or more years for the effects of exposure to be seen, and those who had been exposed to asbestos at a early age were more likely to contract these diseases than those who were first exposed later on in life.

Smokers have a much greater chance of contracting asbestos related diseases than non smokers because

the small hairs and lining of the throat are burned
out, not allowing them to catch incoming asbestos
fibers which could then be spit out and expelled.

During the day, Chief could see eyes glazing over with all the information
brought to light; the Who, What, When, Where, Why and How of asbestos
and lead based paint. Chief was amazed at how unwittingly unconcerned
people can be in the face of information that intimately and critically involves
their health. He knew it was necessary and was determined to circulate all
this information, so at the end of the day clear conclusions could be made.
The stimulating solutions to come would perk the crowd up.

The next person on the asbestos panel to present was Shane Blade, a hero's
hero, a retired NYC firefighter who was present at the World Trade Center
on 9/11 and rescued people during the collapse of the Twin Towers.

Shane was in his early thirties, but looked to be in his late fifties. He
was tall and thin, and his jet-black hair was highlighted with natural, bold
silver streaks. His breathing was short punctuated periodically by coughs,
but his eyes were strong, showing signs of suffering, coupled with what
some interpreted as incredible wisdom, although to him he was just an
ordinary guy who was trying to do what he thought was right. He was
retired because he had health issues, serious respiratory conditions caused
from the extensive exposure he experienced from the weeks working at
Ground Zero. As he cleared his throat before speaking, the room seemed to
lean in a bit to hear the hero speak.

> Asbestos is the best fireproofing known to man, there
> has never been an equal to it! It's saved countless
> more lives than it has ever taken, and in my book, it
> is a firefighter's best friend. It was the second most
> important high-rise building component, next to
> the elevator.

He paused for a breath and a quick cough before continuing.

> Without the invention of the elevator, we would
> never have been able to build high rise skyscrapers.

It's not practical or in some cases physically possible to walk up and down several flights of stairs two to three times a day.

First and foremost, asbestos gave building occupants more time to escape in cases of fire. Secondly, it protects the structural steel from warping during exposure to the high heat given off during a fire. It was used to protect the structural steel of buildings, meeting building code requirements to delay the steel from melting for up to four hours. These four hours would give firefighters enough time to get in the building and do their job of saving lives. If everything else in the building was lost, at least the structural steel, the most expensive component of the building, remained intact. All the rubble could be removed and you could go back in and tack everything back on to the structural steel. Asbestos, first and foremost, can save lives, and secondly, time and money.

Shane made the legitimate argument that if the structural steel on the higher floors of the Twin Towers had been properly coated with asbestos-containing spray-on fireproofing, like the lower floors, they may be standing today, along with his brethren and the thousands of other lost lives, but that was not the case.

These last words seemed more a reminder to himself than part of his testimony, and a glimmer of loss and sorrow graced his eyes before a cough and his continuation.

In 1971 during the middle of the Twin Towers' construction, New York City banned the use of asbestos. Thus, spray-on asbestos fireproofing was only used up to the 64th floor. From the 65th floor on up, the spray-on asbestos fireproofing was replaced by another material that passed Underwriters Laboratories tests, but that many experts believed to be inferior and had to be applied at much higher thicknesses to achieve protection similar to those of asbestos.

He coughed, had a sip of water and continued.

> As we all know, on September 11th, two hijacked planes exploded into the Twin Towers, the first into floors 96 through 103 of Tower One and the other into floors 87 through 93 of Tower Two. According to building codes, asbestos replacement was supposed to give four hours of protection to the structural steel framing before melting. Tower One World Trade Center lasted only one hour and forty minutes, and Tower Two World Trade Center collapsed after a mere 56 minutes.

He paused again for what seemed like a moment of reflection. Maybe he was just catching his breath, but the pause had a certain reverence to it.

> We paid a horrible price for the premature collapse of the towers, with the loss of thousands of lives, including our brave police officers, rescue workers, and firefighters, who lost their lives in the quest to save others. Some of us are still paying that price, including the average citizen who rose to the occasion to try and help his fellow man.

The light started to flash on his table, and Chief signaled to stop it and let him talk. It was one of the most poignant moments of the day: the hero speaking and the unyielding Chief breaking his own rules.

Shane finished up by, saying,

> The irony here was that eight thousand gallons of a green coating material had been used to coat over half a million square feet of the exposed asbestos in the loading docks of the towers, rendering it safe in the presence of the extensive daily work

activities, causing it to never have to be removed or replaced, saving time, the environment, and money. The asbestos fireproofing was there doing its job, as it was originally intended, so that I could do mine—both doing the same job saving lives! If a high profile project like the Twin Towers could benefit from the in-place management of asbestos through green coatings, then it should be greatly considered as the first option and most preferred abatement method on all projects, large or small.

As the hero firefighters' testimony came to a close, there was an instinctive moment of silence before the next panelist began. Chief had decided early on during panel selection that he wanted someone from outside the USA to speak, making everyone aware that these challenges were global and not limited to the United States.

Chief had chosen an outspoken Japanese environmentalist, who opened with a startling statement that currently, in Japan, 20 percent of the homes use asbestos roof tiles. That's some 5 million homes in his country. Most of these tiles were made by one company, which produced the tiles from 1961 to 2001. The bulk of the rest were produced by a second company, from 1971 to 2003. These two companies alone made 600 million of these tiles. When shattered, they have the potential to immediately release enormous amounts of asbestos. Over time, these tiles weather and age and release the asbestos fibers.

These tiles contain 25 percent asbestos, one fourth of the tile's composition, and became popular due to their light weight and the reduced risk of damage during the typhoons and earthquakes that generally plague Japan.

About 4 million of these homes are still in use today, which means that roughly one million of these homes, with their 25 percent asbestos roofs have been demolished, using no means of safe removal, transportation, disposal, or storage.

He spoke of the limited landfills that could handle asbestos. There are a total of six in all of Japan, and none on the island of Okinawa. This means the materials are often shipped to other countries that sometimes don't have a high regard for human life, especially the working or lower classes.

He went into depth, explaining how a lot of people were experiencing the adverse effects of asbestos in proximity to asbestos plants and how their exposure, due to living around them, was now undeniable.

He threw in the fact that asbestos was just recently outlawed in Japan in 2006, and lead-based paint is still manufactured and widely used. He concluded by rattling off some scary statistics about his fellow countrymen, as well as on people in other countries who were being unnecessarily exposed. He also explained how the environment was being damaged for generations to come. In the end, he reasoned that there were simple solutions to this global challenge.

The last panelist of the group was an industrial hygienist from a well-known environmental company, and she spoke about the complications and dangers of hazardous waste generation, transportation, and storage. The major point she brought out was that, whether these materials were in your building or stored in a dump you still had ownership and liability of them, commonly known as cradle to grave or womb to tomb.

She explained that even when the material had been removed from a building it was forever the property of the building owner. She said if the landfill owner decided to move his dump or if there was a clean-up needed due to other materials that were stored in that landfill, the proprietor could send you a bill for your portion, adding to the already costly and often unnecessary process. She also had lots of chilling statistics on how much of these materials were out there and our limited options on dealing with them.

Chief looked around the room. The Day was moving along without a hitch. The panelists were presenting their data in a timely manner, with no problems, all was well ... or so it seemed.

The remaining members of the Chief's panel were still not in attendance; the Chief's assistants were unable to get in contact with Lyn and Marcos. In this day and age of cell phones, email, and blackberries, the idea of not being able to contact someone was the equivalent of them having fallen off the ends of the earth. *Where were they? Did they catch their flight? Were they alright?* The Day marched on. As the panelist finished up, the table's light went out and the room cleared as everyone headed to lunch.

———

CHAPTER 8

Lunch 1200 – 1300

As Chief sat drinking his protein shake, he thought about the facts presented on asbestos, its first and many subsequent uses and the benefits that came from it. He also thought of the easily prevented health concerns associated with it, what a remarkable building material it really was, and how the panic of its potential problems and the push for removal was being so over-blown. Chief reflected on how he had learned the hard way about the continuing ownership of hazardous materials, even after they were removed from a building or property.

Three years after he had asbestos unnecessarily removed from one of his buildings, he started receiving bills from the dump to maintain these materials where he had stored them in a landfill under someone else's control. By the time he had learned about in-place management and that the need to have these materials removed was unnecessary, he had already spent millions of dollars that could have been better spent.

Not only were the materials removed and replaced at a great cost but materials that replaced the asbestos were inferior, and at the very least, questionable. The sad irony was that the replacement materials over time were breaking down and falling off, needing to be sealed to stop their release with the same process and coatings that should have been used to cover up the original asbestos. This, coupled with the fact that the building owner still had the ownership and liability of these materials, was a double whammy. There was no time limit to one's ownership, even years after having had disposed of them.

Why would anyone want to assume these liabilities unless it was absolutely necessary? That information was rarely disclosed at the time of discussing project options. If it was Chief, he would have decided differently on the projects for which he was responsible.

Chief's thoughts were interrupted as one of his anxious assistants brought him the news of the whereabouts of Lyn and Marcos, or rather, the lack thereof. They knew how important their appearance was and nervously said that they were scheduled to fly out of New York earlier that morning, but if the weather in New York was anything like that of Washington, their flight may be delayed, if not canceled altogether. Chief, with poise true to form, told the assistant to stay calm. He was confident that they would make it on time and keep him abreast of any developments.

———

CHAPTER 9

Lead Based Paint

"The Day" marched on and the first panel after lunch started with what some considered more exciting facts. 300 MTG. Tick Tock.

The lead scientist began.

Humans have used lead since the dawn of civilization because of its availability, ease of extraction, and ease of use. It is a highly malleable and ductile metal, and is easy to smelt. There is evidence of its use in the early Bronze Age, where it was used with antimony and arsenic, and was mentioned in the Book of Exodus. Ancient alchemists thought that lead was the oldest metal and associated it with the planet Saturn. Lead's symbol, Pb, is an abbreviation of its Latin name plumbum, the same Latin root of the English word "plumbing." Lead is a chemical element on the periodic table symbolized as Pb with the atomic number 82. Lead is a soft, malleable, heavy, and toxic metal. The use of lead as a component of paints dates back to ancient Egypt, Greece and Rome. In the USA, during the first half of the 1900s, lead-based paint was widely acknowledged as the best paint in production due to its durable and washable surface from which germs could be removed easily. Prior to 1940, lead was in just about all paints, and many federal and state government agencies recommended and specified its use.

As the U.S. National Bureau of Standards, Interior Department and Forest Service stated in the 1930s and 1940s, lead pigments were the most important of white pigments and were the very best choice for home owners because it allowed for longer intervals between repaints.

In fact, from the 1920s through the 1940s, the U.S. Federal Government was one of the foremost proponents of the use of lead-based paint. Based on the recommendations of former government paint experts, President Franklin Roosevelt's Public Works Administration had specified the use of lead-based paint for the interior use of fifty or more public housing projects because of the durability it provided.

Despite mounting evidence of the effects of its use, lead was still used in paints in the United States until the danger became too widely known to be ignored. After the 1978 ban, paint manufacturers replaced lead with other ingredients. When the regulations limiting the allowable amounts of lead in paint were implemented in 1978, the use of lead oxide had all but stopped. Many countries began banning lead in residential paints early in the twentieth century. Yet many industrialized countries such as Japan still use lead in paints. This lead-based oil paint is the same paint that gives off high amounts of harmful VOCs, contributing to greenhouse gases and global warming/climate change.

A few of lead's more damaging applications are:

- As a pigment in paints, especially in white, yellow, and red lead-based paints. The lead in these paints has gone on to pollute and poison.

- For plumbing, extensively in use since ancient Roman times; in water mains and service pipes which were used in the USA up until the early 1970s.

As a natural element, lead does not break down in the environment. Once lead has been dispersed and redeposited in the environment, it remains there and can poison generations, unless it is controlled or removed.

Lead poisoning occurs when lead enters the body via tainted water, by eating tainted soil, eating paint chips containing lead, and breathing or swallowing lead dust. Children tend to obtain lead poisoning from eating paint chips, from putting their hands or other objects covered with lead dust in their mouths, and by inhaling lead dust especially during renovations that disturb painted surfaces where household dust can pick up lead from deteriorating lead-based paint. Among the methods of poisoning, lead-dust poses among the greatest threats, due to its subtle method of being easily inhaled, ingested, and unknowingly absorbed.

During normal activities, lead dust can be generated and when renovations are occurring, it is much more extreme. Lead dust can form when lead-based paint is dry scraped, dry sanded, or heated. Dust also forms when painted surfaces bump or rub against each other or other surfaces. Lead dust also appears during natural aging and erosion of surfaces. Lead chips and lead dust can get on surfaces and objects we interact with daily. Settled lead dust can re-enter the air when we vacuum, sweep, or walk through it.

Children with low lead blood levels may not exhibit symptoms and yet are still being exposed to the poisoning. In addition, children who seem healthy can have high levels of lead in their bodies. In an average adult, 10-15 percent of lead that reaches the digestive tract is absorbed. Young children and pregnant women absorb as much as 50 percent more lead than the average adult due to the body's inability to distinguish it during periods of stress and the body's growth demands. Lead exposure is very harmful to young children and babies, even before they are born. As a result of children's bodies absorbing more lead, their brains and nervous systems are more susceptible to its damaging effects. If not detected early, children with high blood lead levels can suffer from:

- Blood and brain disorders

- Damage to the brain and nervous system

- Behavior and learning problems, such as hyperactivity

- Slowed growth

- Hearing problems

- Headaches

- High blood pressure

- Digestive problems

- Nerve disorders

- Memory and concentration problems

- Muscle and joint pain

- Nephropathy

- Nausea

- Insomnia

- Lethargy

- Abdominal pains

- Irritability

- Reduced IQ

- Reduced motor skills development

Adults with high blood lead levels can suffer from all of the above symptoms, plus:

- Difficulties during pregnancy

- Other reproductive problems (in both men and women)

- In severe cases seizure, coma and death

Finally, exposure to lead has been linked to cancer, in children and adults alike.

The panelist went on to talk about how lead-based paint could be identified.

Home test kits for lead are available. Consumers should not however, rely on these tests before doing renovations or to assure their safety. Studies suggest that they are not always accurate and only questionably test what is on the surface. They don't tell what is below the surface, sometimes several layers down. To test for these, a trained professional should be employed, using the more accurate X-ray fluorescence or XRF. They can also do a TCLP (Toxicity Characteristic Leaching Procedure). This is done by removing a physical sample and sending it to a laboratory for analysis to determine the content of lead.

Testing should never be something that's maybe wanted. It's needed, and without it, suspect surfaces should be dealt with as though they are contaminated and be handled accordingly.

As previously stated, lead has been and still is used in various forms and in a number of products. Lead acetate, also known as the sugar of lead was used by the Roman Empire as a sweetener for wine. This is considered by some to have been the cause of the dementia in many of the Roman Emperors, contributing to the cause of the fall of the Roman Empire. The sweetness of lead in any form, especially in paint is a big challenge, since it actually promotes children to put it in their mouths.

Japanese Geisha are another example where lead based make-up is believed to have caused severe illness and death to those who used it.

The concern about lead's role in mental retardation in children and its link to schizophrenia in adults was one of the key factors that brought about its overall reduction of use. While the sale of lead-based paint has been discontinued in several industrialized countries for some time, many older houses still contain substantial amounts of lead-based paint. It is generally recommended that old paint should never be stripped by sanding, as this may generate lead dust which can be inhaled and ingested.

The older your home, the more likely it contains lead-based paint. Many homes built in the U.S. before 1978 have lead-based paint, and while the U.S. federal government banned the use of lead-based paint in homes in 1978, it can still be found in urban, suburban, and city homes across the country. Whether apartment buildings or single-family homes, private or public housing, interior or exterior, deteriorating lead-based paint poses a serious health risk to their occupants, children in particular.

Abatement is intended to lessen the health risk associated with lead-based paint and can involve the covering of the hazardous materials with approved coatings. It can also include enclosing them with hard barriers, or alternatively, removing the entire hazard. Removal includes the extraction of the lead-paint substrate or stripping of just the lead-based paint itself.

Full removal, however, should be generally reserved for limited areas. Paint removal techniques demand high levels of control as well as worker protection. Stripping the lead-based paint also generates significant amounts of hazardous waste, which requires special transportation, disposal, and storage maintenance.

To protect families from lead exposure due to paint, dust, and soil, in 1992, Congress passed the Residential Lead Based Paint Hazard Reduction Act, also known as Title X. Four years later, on March 6, 1996, the Environmental Protection Agency (EPA) in collaboration with the Department of Housing and Urban Development (HUD) published a final rule, "Lead Requirements for Disclosure of Known lead-based paint Hazards in Housing," which requires the disclosure of known information on lead-based paint and lead-based paint hazards before the sale or lease of most housing built before 1978.

The last panel had ended on-time and delivered the quality data experts and scientists were known for. They didn't embellish any of their information, nor did they put anyone to sleep. So far everything was on track except Chief's entire team being present.

The next up was donning a habit. Sister Mary Grace, a "fire and brimstone" former teacher was now the school administrator in one of the local Catholic Schools. Chief never had direct dealings with her, but her name was well known by those in the field of education. A stout, round, tree-trunk of a woman, she stood five feet two and had fiery red, curly hair. While out of place to most, she held her old reliable cell phone with its outdated antenna extended somewhat like a ruler in her hands as she spoke.

Half the room seemed afraid of what she was going to say, and the other half were just afraid of her. The Sister lectured to the room, unnerving some, but Chief had to admit she was making her point. He was reflecting how some of the previous fact speakers were not nearly as stimulating and how the room was now completely alert and paying attention, leaning on her every word.

The sister's yardstick swinging delivery with a touch of fire and brimstone was a clear and frank presentation of lead's devastating health consequences. It was just what the afternoon needed to again emphasize the seriousness of hazards like lead-based paint... also just how uncomplicated the simple solution of in-place-management with green coatings really was. Returning from his thoughts, Chief felt the nun's eyes on him, causing him to refocus and show that he was listening.

He remembered how the nuns were accurate to twenty feet in delivering an eraser or piece of chalk to the head if you were caught spacing out. Chief didn't understand this behavior when he was younger, and yet he later appreciated that their intensity came from a strong desire for all of their students to do well in the world, long after they left the classroom.

The sister continued her passionate lesson type presentation.

> Lead has no biological significance to the human body when it has bonded with blood, proteins, and bones. Lead remains in the blood for several months after it's taken in. It bonds to bones and teeth for thirty-plus years and influences the body's proteins as long as it is in the body.

> Lead poisoning is difficult to diagnose since it is odorless, quietly blending in with harmless household dust and is known as the "silent epidemic"

among many doctors and specialists alike. Children are the most susceptible to lead exposure because of three interacting factors. First, they have more opportunity for contact with lead sources due to their high level of activity. Second, lead absorption occurs more readily in a child compared to adults, mainly because their little bodies try to grab as much nutrition as possible. Lastly, children are still developing and as a result are far more vulnerable to lead than adults. In the U.S. alone, about 900,000 children, ages one to five, have a blood-lead level above the levels of concern. Many believe there is no such thing as a safe exposure limit.

Many of these statements reminded Chief of Rachel Carson's masterpiece "Silent Spring." The nun continued:

Only a small percentage of children who suffer from lead poisoning display obvious symptoms, and while lead poisoning is virtually impossible to diagnose without a blood test, the State Department of Health has noted that some warnings signs include: moodiness or irritability, constipation, short attention span, headaches, fatigue, paleness, change in appetite, joint or muscle pain, and diminished motor skills. Currently the blood lead level is considered safe at 10 Microgram per deciliter (10 ug/dl) or less; however, lower levels have been found to still be harmful. As a result, the Centers for Disease Control and Prevention (CDCP) established in 1991 that 10 ug/dL was an "unsafe" level of lead in blood.

It is currently estimated that 890,000, roughly 4.4 percent of the preschool age children in the United States have a blood level of 10 ug/dl or higher. In northeastern cities, more than 35 percent of the preschool children have blood lead levels that exceed10ug/dl, from exposure to residential lead hazards.

Lead poisoning is the number one environment disease of U.S. children. Of the 20 million children in the United States, almost 9 percent, roughly 1,800,000 have blood lead levels at or above the "level of concern" established by the Center for Disease Control and Prevention. This epidemic of lead poisoning is more widespread than any other preventable childhood disease.

The ingestion of lead dust from contaminated surfaces is the most common pathway of childhood lead poisoning. Due to its small particle size, lead dust can be hard to see and difficult to clean and avoid. Lead dust gets on children's hands, toys, and on other surfaces, and then enters their bodies through normal hand to mouth activities and breathing.

Lead-based paint is the most common source of lead exposure for pre-school children. The primary origin of lead danger is through fine particles of lead-laden dust in the home. Many houses and apartments built before 1978 have paint that contains lead and peeling, decomposing lead paint chips pose a serious health hazards if not properly managed.

The Sister stressed that, contrary to general belief, lead poisoning does not occur merely from eating paint chips generated by deteriorating paint. Lead dust can be absorbed by contact with these and other surfaces that contain lead contaminates.

Dust is generated when paint weathers, deteriorates, erodes, or is disturbed, especially during renovations. This dust can be inhaled, landing in the nose and mouth, then absorbed into the body. This also happens when paint is rubbed off friction-bearing surfaces and pinch points, such as windows, doorways, stairways, and flooring surfaces.

Once again, the point was made that children, especially those ages six and under, are the most susceptible to the harmful effects of lead because of their rate of adsorption is higher at that critical stage of their development.

At low levels, lead poisoning has been proven to decrease IQ points, shorten attention span, cause hyperactivity, aggressive behavior, reading disabilities, and other learning and behavioral problems. At these blood lead levels, below 10ug/dl, the harsher symptoms of poisoning are generally unnoticed. Children with high blood lead levels, however, usually require hospitalization and medical treatment. At very high lead exposure, lead can cause serious permanent damage as a neurotoxin and lead to mental retardation, coma, convulsions, and decreased development of motor skills, cancer, and death.

Lead poisoning is a preventable disease. If lead poisoning can be prevented, the ripple effects of its absence will be visible though the higher birth rate of children, increased test scores from our youth, and a decrease of criminals in a our jails. If nothing is done, the repercussions will reverberate for generations, with mothers passing the lead from their bodies on to that of their unborn children.

Everyone in the room understood the magnitude of lead poisoning and its potentially far reaching effects, well almost everyone. Dracoff sat in the back of the room with a "Where are the violins?" look on his face.

Lastly, the nun strongly stated that we all needed to educate ourselves, which of course was taking place today. As an afterthought, she mentioned that most materials like asbestos and lead-based paint, as well as others such as fiber glass, can be safely managed in-place.

As the sister closed with her concerned and almost scolding tone, it was clear she was very effective, caring and at the same time stern.

The light at her table went out and on at the next table. Chief overheard one of his assistants jokingly say that he was glad she was finished because after the twelve years of Catholic school, even though a long time ago, he "still got nervous being around penguins." Ironically, that humor and his voiced opinions that he should have kept to himself, are what got him the justifiable extra and unwanted attention from the nuns in the first place.

The next panel would present cases of lead poisoning and lead litigation due to lead-based paint exposure. They also addressed a potential conspiracy to cover up the ill effects of the exposure to lead from lead-based paint.

They began: In 1978, the U.S. banned the use of lead-based paint, but due to the excessive use of it before the ban, much of the paints are still in place. They went into great detail about how in the past, both public and private lawsuits were brought up against companies that once manufactured lead-pigment paints designed for residential, commercial, and industrial use, over forty years ago. They also explained how for a lawsuit to be brought the said item had to be "based" on something. For instance, the case must be developed around that item or the most important ingredient in the finished product. In this case, the lawsuit would have to be centered on the lead content of the paint.

Also on this panel was a very credible prominent, former congressman-turned-lobbyist representing some of the larger paint companies that presented a strong argument, backed up with plausible statistics, showing that if there is or was a conspiracy to cover up the dangers of lead-pigmented paint, it lies not with the manufacturers.

He also stated that, to date, none of the former manufacturers of lead pigment paint has ever conspired to conceal the dangers of lead paint. As a matter of fact, in the late 1940s, it was the Lead Industries Association (LIA) that funded the medical research confirming that poorly maintained lead-based paint was the leading source of child exposure to lead. The LIA didn't try to cover up the problem; they sought to publicize it and help alert the public of the dangers of unmaintained lead-pigment paint. On top of this, manufacturers voluntarily adopted a national standard to stop the use of lead pigments in paints intended for interior home use back in 1955, twenty years before the government banned its use.

Chief had one more important panelist, Dr. Zan Dumas, a university Sociology professor who presented some facts dealing with those individuals who were being unfairly exposed when these materials were removed. This issue went way beyond local towns, cities, and states. It was now affecting entire countries.

Dr. Dumas began by stating the obvious that unfair treatment of any kind was wrong.

> Minority, impoverished communities suffer much more exposure to these hazardous materials than rich, affluent ones. The only appropriate term for this kind of environmental discrimination is 'criminal.

> Studies and research had shown that there was environmental racism and economic discrimination at work.

> Environmental discrimination including racial bias is when environmental policymaking is determined by one's race, ethnicity, or economic status. It is discrimination in the enforcement of regulations and laws. It is environmental racial discrimination in the deliberate targeting of individuals, communities, and countries of color. It is also carried over to discriminating the economically disadvantaged as well as countries of color that are economically disadvantaged and targeted for toxic waste disposal and the sitting of polluting industries.

> It is the unfair treatment of a person, group, or country on the basis of prejudice that needs to be acknowledged, addressed and stamped out. It is racial discrimination in the official sanctioning of the life-threatening presence of poisons and pollutants in communities of color. And, it is racial discrimination in the history of excluding

people of color from the mainstream environmental groups, decision making boards, commissions, and regulatory bodies.

Environmental racism, sometimes called environmental injustice, is a modern term used to describe an age-old phenomenon in which people of color and those of lower classes are subjected to environmental and health risks in disproportionately higher numbers than other groups in society.

It is a result of hundreds of years of colonial oppression where the exploitation of people of color, the land, and natural resources are interwoven. In communities where people of color reside and work, there is an increased chance for exposure to toxic landfills, incinerators, industrial dumping, and other environmentally hazardous undertakings.

Many can be said to live in "disposable communities, to be thrown away when the population they hold have outlived their usefulness."

Chief was always upset when he heard these inflammatory statements, and comments like these only confirmed his conviction to help put an end to those practices. She had pointed out that people of color are disproportionately found in industries with "high levels of occupational health risks and in the most hazardous jobs within those and other industries."

These people are somewhat mistakenly considered like the pawns on a chessboard, perceived to be less important and therefore more expendable. In fact they can be very powerful, with strength coming from their numbers, when they bond together for a common cause.

This type of discrimination results in significantly increased occupational disease and mortality rates.

In homes, children of color are exposed to lead at alarming rates. This is partly due to the age and condition of the housing stock, which was once painted with lead-based paint. These children are often trapped in segregated communities, where living conditions are substandard. Environmental pollution caused by deteriorating lead-based paint and additional contaminants have given rise to an epidemic of childhood asthma and other respiratory diseases.

Asthma is the most common illness among children in separated communities. Many cities and towns still practice de-facto segregation, even if it is no longer a matter of official public policy. Numerous children struggle to breathe. Some mothers keep oxygen tanks next to their beds, which the kids refer to as "breathing machines." U.S. Native American reservations and Third World nations alike suffer a similar fate. These communities and nations are more and more being targeted as dumping grounds for unwanted hazardous waste.

In the U.S., the concept of social pollution has assisted in segregating people of color, particularly people of African descent, from the majority of people in society because they appear as threats to the structure and organizing principles of social order. The central characteristic of this concept is the attribution, by the majority culture, of socially unacceptable behaviors (which the majority culture actually exhibits) to a particular group of people. Segregation of the races was perpetuated and is still perpetuated to this day. This results in what has been referred to as "residential apartheid." It maintains that apartheid-type housing and urban development policies deliberately limit mobility, reduce neighborhood options, and diminish job opportunities for millions of Americans, particularly African-Americans who are unjustly more likely to live in racially segregated communities, regardless of income. "In 1990, more than 57 percent of African Americans lived in central cities, the highest concentration of any racial and ethnic group."

It has been brought to light that regardless of income, education, or professional achievement, some minorities are exposed to higher crime rates, less effective educational systems, high mortality risks, more dilapidated surroundings, and greater environmental threats because of their race. Institutional barriers make it difficult for many households to buy their way out of health-threatening physical environments.

As a result of unfair marketing practices and unjust governmental policies, millions of African Americans have been segregated from other Americans into geographically isolated areas that are economically depressed and polluted urban neighborhoods. These communities have been perceived by some as an "appropriately polluted space" because the people who reside in these communities are perceived by the larger culture as socially polluted. The pollution here is less visible and poses very little risk to the white community. Therefore, it is not by coincidence that people of color are subjected to such environmental ills, many times being a matter of public policy.

What about all these children?

Depression is common among children in communities that are environmentally distressed. Many cry a great deal but cannot explain exactly why. Fear and anxiety are common, and many cannot sleep.

One cannot help but wonder, with a great amount of dread, what psychological affect this type of environment has on its tiny victims. The physical affects mentioned are well documented and devastating enough. These children cannot help but compare their environment to the beautiful, splendid home images portrayed on television as the typical American landscape. The contrast must be striking, shocking, and confusing. They must wonder why they are subjected to such squalor, pollution, disease, hopelessness, and violence.

This does have a profound affect on their social, educational, and physical development. They cannot help but feel they are not valued in this society, because to many, they are not. Societies have developed a very effective system that will trap many of them in a state of confusion, hopelessness, rage, and sickness, well into adulthood.

This is the tragedy of class distinction, environmental racism, and economic discrimination. Children are essentially sentenced to life imprisonment without the possibility of parole, not because they have committed any crime, but because of their skin color and class, which brands them as subhuman and not deserving of the same rights as the larger culture in our society.

The panelist making her point deliberately made other bold statements that caused most of the people in attendance to cringe.

It's amazing that many of the same people in the ruling class in any society who practice race and class segregation consider themselves an example for the rest of civilization.

The Environmental Justice Movement in the U.S., coming from a historical perspective states that during the 1970s, higher educational institutions and civil rights groups noted the inconsistencies in environmental health protection. There were studies that cited written reports during this period identified inequities from air and hazardous waste pollution.

Most of the studies' concerns fell on deaf ears until 1982 when residents of Warren County, North Carolina successfully blocked a landfill marked for the disposal of soil contaminated by PCB. The governor selected an alternative site for the landfill, Afton, whose inhabitants were 84 percent black. Warren County was 64 percent black, and the state of North Carolina was only 24 percent black. In addition to this, many scientists noted that the Afton site was problematic because the water table was close to the ground surface and many residents relied on wells as their source of water. The potential for contamination was high. Opposition by grassroots organizations followed. During this nonviolent protest, four hundred people were arrested.

This incident influenced Walter Fauntroy, District of Columbia's Congressional Delegate, to call for the investigations of hazardous waste facilities in EPA Region IV. It was found that "while blacks represented 20 percent of Region IV's population, in communities surrounding three of the four commercial landfills in Region IV, blacks comprised more than 50 percent of the population.

During the 1980s, other researchers investigated this issue of inequity in environmental protection. Robert Bullard, a sociologist and a leader in this field, authored *Dumping in Dixie,* in which he investigated the issue of waste facilities in five southern black communities and how the residents addressed this problem. He and other researchers were instrumental in stirring interest in this subject and putting environmental injustice on the national agenda.

In 1986 the United Church of Christ conducted a study of the correlation of race and income to the location of hazardous waste sites. It concluded that race was "the most significant variable in determining the location of a commercial hazardous waste facility.

In January of 1990, a Conference on Race and the Incidence of Environmental Hazards was held at the University of Michigan, sponsored by the civil rights organizations and the academic community. One group of presenters, referred to as the Michigan Coalition, wrote to a number of government agencies and congressman and demanded action on this issue.

In July of the same year, EPA Administrator William Reilly formulated the Environmental Equity Workgroup to ascertain the extent of the problem and to recommend possible solutions. Because the EPA had not collected data regarding environmental protection in regards to race and income, it was difficult for this group to get substantial data regarding this issue. It, however, did indicate there were trends that supported arguments by earlier researchers. The work group recommended that the EPA do the following: collect data based on race and socioeconomic status and take this information into consideration when making risk assessment and risk management decisions; target high risk communities and institute measures to reduce environmental risks; "promote the use of equity considerations in the rule making process as well as all agency permit, grant, and compliance monitoring and enforcement procedures;" enhance communication with people of color and impoverished communities as well as including these entities in the decision making process; finally the EPA needed to "address equity in its long-term strategic plan."

In 1991, the First National People of Color Environmental Leadership Summit was held in Washington D.C. This resulted in the adoption of the Principles of Environmental Justice. Some key concepts included but are not limited to: "respect for the earth, freedom from environmental discrimination, right to a balanced and ethical use of land, self determination, accountability for the production and handling of hazardous materials, right to participation in the decision making about one's environment, the right to a safe and secure workplace, compensation for damage, restoration of cities in balance with nature, honoring the cultural integrity of the neighborhoods, and providing access to a full range of resources, informed consent, and education based on appreciation of diverse cultural perspectives.

It was crystal clear to many participants that the link between environmental justice and the urban environment required immediate attention and action.

The main thrust of the environmental justice movement is towards urban reconstruction. Cities must be valued as distinct centers for racial and cultural diversity and exchange. Rebuilding urban centers presents employment opportunities and other opportunities for economic development. This economic development must include the inner city communities, organizations, and enterprises in every aspect of the planning and decision making process. More energy efficient, non-polluting, green solutions must be promoted to our existing housing stock. Urban centers must develop links to each other, becoming politically more powerful, thus allowing them to set their own environmental policy agendas.

We also must green our existing schools and facilities making them safe and health code compliant. Most of these buildings only have to have hazards brought under control, with simple solutions bringing them up to code. We found out that asbestos and lead-based paint only had to be abated, not removed.

The lead panels were finished and the information on both asbestos and lead made it clear that these materials were present in our daily lives. If not properly managed, they could and would wreak havoc on everyone exposed to them.

It was now getting close to the good part of the day where the simple solutions for these sometimes complicated issues were going to be presented. Yet, there were still two obstacles to overcome: Dracoff's panel was yet to present, and Lyn and Marcos had not shown up.

Dracoff's panel consisted of an unwitting nurse, a landlord and a devious attorney. Chief was sure the attorney would twist the facts in Dracoff's favor. Dracoff owned several companies; one, of course, was a hazardous material removal company, another dealt in hazardous landfills, and another was a hazardous material trucking company. He was also one of the largest real estate holders in D.C., and by far, the largest slumlord in the United States, owning thousands of low income units.

Dracoff and his despicable business cronies planned to come out the winner, whether there was total removal or nothing done at all. He was really pushing for full removal, which would benefit his companies, and his wallet, the most. Wrongly, as far as he saw it, there was no real way to make money with in-place management. It required things like good customer service, quality products, and warranties, all of which he avoided, seeing them as costly and pointless.

Dracoff's ultimate goal was that of planned obsolescence. Even though he understood that in-place management would be best for all, Dracoff would fight it all the way to the bank, or so he would hope. There was always a way of spinning things in one direction or another, and he was an expert at such, and the Chief suspected his team would be as well.

The genius was that two of Dracoff's panel members were just pawns, not knowing they were doing or expressing anything wrong. They truly believed what they were saying, for better or worse, and unfortunately, regardless of who suffered. They sincerely believed that if you could not remove all of the asbestos or lead based paint that there was no point in trying to remove any of it or to control it. This was not an uncommon thought process.

The existence of websites such as the one about vermiculite clearly stated and spread this "remove it or do nothing" mentality. Dracoff's panel proposal would be either to leave the hazard alone or to completely remove it. If it was decided to leave the hazards alone, there would be no excess cost to him on any of his buildings. If removal was mandated, they would push for governmental subsidizing, due to the fact that individual landlords and homeowners could never afford to have all the hazards completely removed. The attorney would state that the only way to protect people from being exposed was to fully remove the hazards, and that the landlords should receive government subsidies. Either way, in Dracoff's mind, he would win.

Before the table light of the last panel turned off, Chief looked down at his watch. There was 120 MTG, and most of The Day had already passed. There had been panels presenting on everything from the history and make-up of asbestos and lead-based paint to the health ramifications and documented cases of the poisonous effects of both, and only the last panel had touched on the simple solution.

At this point, The Day had been like many similar deliberations the Chief had taken part in: plenty of talk yet no action. There were discussions of what could be causing problems, testing for problems, the "discovery of problems," and no presented solutions. Thousands of dollars (Cha-Ching), hundreds of man-hours wasted (Tick Tock), and no conclusions on how to help our children and families secure our future or protect our environment (Whoosh). This wasn't one of those days, however; this was Chief's day, the day the good guys would prevail. But there were still miles to go.

Chief's panel was still short two members, and Otis, at times, was badly perspiring. There were times during the other panel's presentations when Chief got the impression that Otis was about to jump out of his seat and scream, "Just encase it!" but he had controlled himself.

Chief wasn't a worrying man, he was calculating and logical. However, the absence of two of his trio just did not seem to add up. Dracoff's vulture-like smirk, while looking from Chief to Otis, began to make Chief wonder if he had something to do with their absence. *But how could he?* How could he know the connection between them and Chief? At this point it was all speculation, and he would have to wait to see the end results.

———

CHAPTER 10

Dracoff's Pawns

The table light for Dracoff's panel came on. Chief looked at the group with mild concern. It wasn't the panel that concerned him but who the panel might unrighteously convince or appeal to with the do nothing or remove it all approach to these potentially hazardous materials.

This was Chief's main reason for timing his panel last, providing the powerful close, after all the facts were presented. As long as those who listened to or watched The Day's recorded tapes were sensible enough to know this, Chief knew they would see simple in-place management as the way of dealing with over 90 percent of lead-based paint and asbestos challenges, as well as being the pro-planet solution. Nonetheless, the game was afoot, and Chief knew that Dracoff was maliciously intelligent and that he would certainly not appeal to those in need, but to those in power.

At this point, the panel was composed of:

- A Registered Nurse who was also a misled parent, driven to the point of fanaticism by the debilitating effect lead-based paint had taken on her child.

- A low rent landlord who had been cleaned up and was truly in a tough spot due to these potentially hazardous materials.

The Mastermind cunning enough to put these two obvious foes together was none other than Dracoff's own...

- Head attorney who with his waxed mustache and contemptuous scornful sneer closely resembled Snidely Whiplash.

On a good day, Chief wouldn't have batted an eye at Dracoff's supporting cast, but today his team was short by two. Chief's assistants were able to update him that Lyn arrived in New York City the night before. She had met up with Marcos, and they were supposed to fly to Washington this morning. Due to a snowstorm in New York, flights had been delayed, and there was no telling whether they would make it in on time. As information trickled in, it was believed that Marcos had made the decision to have a driver take them to Washington, but no one had heard from them since. On this blustery day, Chief had to admit, Dracoff's team was looking to have the potential of swaying everyone toward the remove it all or do nothing strategy.

The first panelist was a mother of three, a nurse, and an African-American. However, today, she was presented as a nurse first, a mother second, and an African-American last.

> Now we've all heard the experts talk about asbestos and lead-based paint for most of the day. You've talked about what these hazardous materials are made of, where they come from, what they are used for, and why they were used. We've even heard how greatly they insulate, how durable they are, and all in all, how useful they are. Lastly, we've heard of the hazardous effects of asbestos and lead-based paint. Why is it that it took all the experts so long to find out the negative effects of these materials if the ancient Greeks knew about it?

Chief had to admit that she had a strong point. The simple answer was that, like other hazards we coexist with on a daily basis, the good out-weighed the bad. However, it was neither the time nor the place for refutes.

> Now we've all been brought here to present the facts, and I'd like to point out a couple of them myself. In the northeastern part of this country, over 35 percent of the preschool children have blood lead levels above the 10ug/dl safe limit due to exposure from residential lead hazards. The average blood lead levels increased in African-American and Latino children as their poverty levels increased.

The most important fact, and I'm sure all parents will agree, is that we don't give a damn about all your tests and reasons. We want to know how to protect our children and loved ones, since you all (pointing to the previous panels) can't figure it out. We as parents have a simple solution. We want it gone! Remove it all. Remove it and guarantee that no else is ever exposed or tortured with the harmful effects of unnecessary exposure.

We've always been told by the specialists and experts not to let our children eat paint chips, and like any caring parent, we listened because you're the experts. So we ignored the dust from the chipped, peeling, delaminating paint and concentrated on making sure our kids didn't put chips in their mouths. We sweep up the bits that fall off, but our children still get sick, and you experts do your testing and tell us again not to let our children eat paint chips. Sometimes, we even scold our children again, telling them not to eat the chips, listening to the experts.

Some of our children start getting complaints from school for poor behavior: they're not listening in class and are often sleepy and irritable. They get placed in special education classes. Our children start getting sicker, and they complain of occasional stomach pains and headaches, so we take them to the doctors, who after doing blood tests, say that our children are suffering from lead poisoning and ask us about our insurance coverage. We can't afford the needed treatment, so we are told to 'keep them at home, let it run its course, keep them away from paint chips, and make sure they get plenty of fresh air.' We place them next to windows, the same windows that are always mysteriously dusty, and then the light goes on. We do our own research and find that windows are where the highest concentration levels of lead dust can sometimes be found.

We ask our landlords to do something about the asbestos and lead base paint. We get different versions of the same 'do nothing, stall tactics,' such as 'we are working on getting it resolved,' or 'we've taken it under advisement, we can't afford to address the issue.' We look to the law, and they tell us there are few successful cases dealing with lead-based paint problems and that there are limited laws on these issues. Well, our children and loved ones aren't issues! They are our families and loved ones. So I'm here today representing the parents and the people and families of children to make the lawmakers do something."

Chief listened to her case and her plight; unfortunately he had heard it all before. The sad fact was that it was common for unethical professionals to mislead clients on the dangers of asbestos and lead-based paint. It's difficult to get a man to understand something or do the right thing if his salary depends on him not understanding it.

Cha-Ching.

Aside from the potential danger of asbestos and lead-based paint hazards, the problem was funding. Chief had been part of projects dealing with total asbestos and lead-based paint removal and replacement. The fact was that it was too costly in every way (TEM). As Chief observed the nurse's agitated tone he wondered if Dracoff was concerned with the time they had left and glanced over at him to check. To his surprise, Dracoff was still looking confident; that's when it hit the Chief: Dracoff wasn't concerned with the facts, the time, or even the nurse and her family's suffering. He was ultimately concerned with the overall performance, especially after half a day of hearing what he considered to be the pencil pushers and note takers delivering facts and figures. The emotional pleas of the nurse shouting to "Remove it all, make sure every bit is gone, and take it completely away!" was sure to leave a mark. Genius. Chief couldn't help but wonder why Dracoff never used his intelligence for good. He had so many opportunities to do so.

Chief saw millions of dollars wasted on the unnecessary removal and replacement of asbestos and lead-based paint. He was able to save sometimes as much as 94 percent on in-place management projects over the direct costs of removal and replacement. He was able to do more projects with in-place management, it being value engineering at its best.

A minute before her time was up, the attorney signaled to the RN, who concluded with,

> It's our obligation as parents to care and provide for our families and the environment in which they live. We live in these homes, so the decision should be ours to make. We want the asbestos, lead-based paint and any of the other hazards that can harm our children and families removed. Our children and loved ones have the right to a decent and healthy life. Remove it!

At the RN's conclusion Otis thought how impossible her suggestion really was, comparing it to removing all the other hazards (electricity, gasoline, water, and fire) from our lives.

Chief heard her argument and knew it wasn't practical, especially since a lot of these materials were still being manufactured and used in other parts of the world.

The landlord was up next and he began to speak.

> I too know the deadly effects of asbestos and lead-based paint. Some believe that we, the landlords, are heartless--that we refuse to take action for the love of money. But it's not our love of money that ties our hands; it's our lack of money. I have three apartment buildings laden with asbestos and lead-based paint. My father bought these building in early 1960s and handed them down to me. I had

no idea about asbestos and lead-based paint issues, and neither did he. He always told me to take care of the tenants, and that's what I try to do. Some believe that laws should be made to have asbestos and lead-based paint completely removed, and to this, I can't help but ask: who's going to pay for it?

The room was silent.

The average cost to remove asbestos and lead-based paint from a building can far exceed the total cost of the building, and that cost doesn't include the transportation, storage, and replacement of these potential hazardous materials. Once again, I ask: who is going to pay for that? Here is a fact that may open the eyes of the 'removal hound.'

After WWII, in 1943, the federal government established rent control so that the troops returning home could afford housing. In order for building and homeowners to afford insurance, maintenance, and to make any profit, the federal government subsidized much of the rent. In the city of New York, this didn't happen. Rent control was implemented, but it was unsubsidized. Dozens of owners abandoned the buildings, unable to afford and maintain their buildings due to the lack of subsidizing. Approximately 300,000 units were given up.

He stated that if removal laws are passed forcing the building owners to remove all their asbestos and lead-based paint, history would only repeat itself. He said that three of his apartment buildings were low-income apartments and he was barely making enough to keep the building running and provide for his family.

If a law is made forcing me to remove all the asbestos and lead-based paint in my three buildings, I will have no choice but to claim bankruptcy and abandon the buildings.

I know no one wants to hear this, but either the government aids building owners in the full removal of these hazards, or they do nothing and leave us alone.

Chief was thinking that so many more projects could be done at a much faster and economical rate with management in-place techniques. So much more bang for the buck. Cha-Ching.

The only time in-place management may not be a fit would be in the case of a demolition or a remodel, and then the hazardous material should be handled accordingly. Any other time, these materials should not be disturbed and management in-place methods should be utilized.

Chief knew what he was talking about and also knew what Dracoff was trying to do with his unsuspecting panel. He was trying to focus on removal being the only option and using it as a means of delaying any action being taken at all. This didn't bother the Chief. He knew once his team arrived that they would torpedo that argument. The challenge was getting them there.

The first two panelists had managed to use the right amount of theatrics and time to leave Dracoff's Attorney 20 MTG for his statements. The Chief thought that if Dracoff had a son, this attorney would fit the bill.

He began.

I believe that the problems faced by our own panel are proof of the problems faced by the governors of our states, the citizens of our cities, and the members of our communities. Asbestos and lead-based paint are hazards to one and all. All of the facts have revealed this, and the reason that we are here today is to find a solution. We have two clear options: On one side, we have total and complete removal. If laws were put into place to make this mandatory no one would suffer from the diseases caused by asbestos and lead-based paint exposure. We would never have to worry about our children or loved ones being affected by these diseases, caused by simply living in their very own homes. The home is a place where we should all feel safe, a place we should never have to worry about the monsters that lurk within.

Otis squirmed as he listened to the attorney's self-serving babble. He continued,

This is why we propose that a law should be made to have all asbestos and lead-based paint removed, but not at the cost to the building owners. Nationwide, HUD anticipates the costs associated with the new regulations to be about $564 million, while the benefits are anticipated to hit $2.65 billion. These benefits include the improved lifetime earnings of children saved from lead poisoning, reduced medical and special education, reduced juvenile delinquency and related costs on the education system, and reduced personal injury claims.

According to the estimates made by HUD, approximately 57 million pre-1978 housing units contain some lead based paint. Over half of the nation's entire housing stock. In general, the older the housing, the greater the amount of lead-based paint.

Chief focused his attention on the attorney as one of his assistants continually attempted to reach Lyn and Marcos. It seemed, however, that all of the systems were down due to the storm. The Chief didn't know if his expert panel would arrive in time. He was counting on them being there and could only imagine how uncomfortable it would be for everyone to watch Otis sweat and stutter through the last and most important sixty minutes, without aid. The Chief visualized an intervention.

The Attorney continued with more facts and figures, backing up the argument of how total removal was the only way to fully prevent exposure to loved ones. He claimed it was necessary and that the only way to accomplish it was with government subsidizing the removal, replacement, transportation, and storage of the unwanted waste.

As Dracoff's lawyer began drawing to a close and the light at his table began to flash, Chief couldn't help but feel a bit uneasy for Otis. He had been there all day, awaiting his turn to present. At times, he seemed fit to explode over the misinformation that was being delivered. At other times he was much too nervous to look up from his hands at all. At this moment though, Otis was anything but nervous. The Day had taken its toll on him, and he had come out the better for it. Otis was more ready than ever to deliver on the facts.

In contemplation of all that was said throughout the day, it had become clearer to Otis what he needed to do. It was sometime after lunch that Chief started noticing the change in him. There were so many misconceptions stated that provoked Otis to want to speak out of turn, but he fought the urge, time and again, and held his tongue. He understood the importance of all the correct information being disseminated to all the right people.

It was only moments before his presentation and the more the attorney said the more Otis got fired up. He could not wait to present the facts. Otis seemed to possess the steel resolve Chief had hoped The Day would have on everyone who participated. As a backup, Chief had planned to have two of his assistants present the information Liz and Marcos had prepared. Primarily, the intention was to lessen the pressure on Otis, but looking at him, Chief knew that the act would only insult the man.

As the Chief diverted his attention once again to the center of the room, he spotted the remaining members of his stunning A-team. Lyn and Marcos had blazed into the room, removed their coats, and had begun to march to their assigned seats. Otis, relieved and just slightly disappointed that he would not have to deliver their findings along with his own, looked at them, smiled, and began his presentation.

———

CHAPTER 11

Chief's Champions

<u>Otis the Passionate</u> opened in the same way he had for years, strongly stating that in-place management with green coatings was the most cost effective, safe, and sane way to deal with asbestos, lead-based paint, and other hazardous building materials, as well as, extending and preserving all building components.

He went on to state that for some reason, "There is a general misconception regarding asbestos that there was some law already in place concerning the mandatory removal of asbestos in buildings. The truth of the matter is that there has never been nor will there ever be such a law. What is required, however, is that clean air and safe conditions be provided for all buildings occupants. The process in which this task is accomplished is primarily the building owner's responsibility.

The industry use of the term abatement seems to have lead to more confusion. Most people, including a lot of industry experts, often confused the term abatement with full-blown removal. Abatement, though, means to decrease in the amount, intensity, or degree of something--to cut it back, to cover it up, to seal it in, to encase, or to stop the release of. This definition, then, would include the process for in-place management of asbestos and lead-based paint.

Removal and replacement, being the most expensive options, should be considered only as a final alternative. Notice that I didn't say the 'safest' option. While removal does decrease the chance of exposure in the long run, it increases the chances of exposure during removal, to the removal contractors and to the general public. Asbestos and lead-based paint cannot be removed without residual particles being left behind, which can then later be released, causing the same problem they were removed to prevent.

The best method of in-place management is with industrial, green protective coatings. They should be used to contain and safely manage these potential hazards in place, before the hazard needs to be replaced. As previously mentioned with the case of asbestos, there is no known equal substitute material that applied at the same thickness that could equal the fireproofing and fire resistance characteristics of asbestos.

Let's look at this from another angle: water, fire, electricity, and gasoline are all invaluable in our present way of life, yet they are also all hazards, in one way or another. We've become so accustomed to safely managing them in-place that one probably can't even see them for what they are: potential hazards. People die daily from each of these hazards—be it via electrocution, asphyxia, drowning, fire, or explosion. They are all hazards, and even more so, they are hazards that have been managed in-place.

This being the case, when it comes to asbestos and lead-based paint, the question isn't whether to remove or not but how they can be safely managed in-place to continue to do what they were originally intended to do.

Without the proper in-place management, hazards such as electricity in this very building, the gas and water lines in our homes and work places, and the gasoline in our vehicles would all be horrendous, life threatening materials, making the uses of these greatly important necessities infeasible. Without the proper coatings used on electric wires, people would die by electrocution daily. Without in-place management of potentially hazardous material, our homes would blow-up and flood regularly, and our gas filled vehicles would be bombs on wheels, ready to detonate. How is it that we have managed to forget and overlook these hazards so easily? It's because all of these potential hazards have been safely managed in-place.

The same can be done with asbestos and lead-based paint. Most people do not like to use inferior products, and as a worker in the trades, I can tell you that there is no equal to asbestos. So then why not coat it to protect ourselves, and let the superior product do the job it was originally intended to do?

Chief watched as the simple logic surprised most people and began to sink in. They had never thought of it that way, although it made perfect sense, and it surely made no sense to remove and replace all of these materials when they were still effectively doing what they were supposed to do.

When I talk about coatings, I don't mean slapping on a coat of any old, cheap paint. This is why in-place management with coatings has been misunderstood and at times gotten a bad reputation in the industry. Materials have been used where they shouldn't, and cheap materials were used when only quality ones would be effective.

Cheap coatings should never be considered when it comes to covering hazardous materials. As with other hazardous materials that have been managed in-place all around us, quality is what matters. We wouldn't want a cheap coating to be used over our electric cords or cheap materials to be used in making the lines that are used for bringing gas into our homes or work places, and certainly not the use of cheap gasoline tanks for our vehicles.

Otis always enjoyed using the example of skydiving and having the choice of a cheap parachute or a quality one. He laughed at the ridiculousness of it because to him it was certainly a no brainer. He, like all the people he asked this question to, would always demand the quality one.

It's the same thing with a gasoline tank or the coating over our electric cords: quality matters. We want quality, and it should be the same for the in-place management of asbestos and lead-based paint.

We should never use cheap materials over asbestos or lead-based paint. Quality green coatings aren't expensive; they are priceless. It is simply the difference between price of a product used today and the overall cost of it in the long term.

There are several requirements quality coatings should posses: They should first be green, environmentally friendly, water based, and not have any harmful or adverse effects on people or the environment. These coatings should be proven to be so clean and safe that they can even be applied with pregnant women and children present.

They should, therefore, have minimal VOCs (Volatile Organic Content) and no ODS (Ozone Depleting Substances). This is a big consideration with the use of green coatings on projects because of the effect VOCs have on the environment.

Naturally, VOCs react with nitrogen oxides in the air when exposed to sunlight to form ozone. In the atmosphere, ozone is beneficial because it absorbs

UV and protects humans, plants, and animals from exposure to dangerous solar radiation that could cause anything from sunburn to skin cancer. In the lower layers of the atmosphere, however, VOCs can cause respiratory problems, crop loss, building damage, and a decline in forestry.

In the upper atmosphere, excessive VOCs perpetuate the greenhouse effect by reducing the amount of heat and solar radiation released by the planet, thus contributing to global warming and climate change.

From my own past projects, I've learned that good intentions can backfire and that solving one problem can result in the creation of another. Case in point: A project in the earlier days of in-place management of a large asbestos project went sour when the product that was used gave off strong VOCs, had a horrible lingering odor, and was extremely flammable as well as explosive in liquid form. This caused the industrial hygienist who was hired to monitor the project to give more concern about the safety of the product that was being used than to the asbestos that was being managed in-place. This product also dried hard, with no elongation, so that it cracked with any building movement.

These specialty coatings should be sustainable and renewable. By this, I mean that they can withstand aging, and over time, as the coatings erode away, another coat of the same material can be applied over top, causing a cross-link bond with itself, leaving a system in which there would never be the need for tearing off or replacing the coating.

Any coatings used should be able to hold up over long periods of time. Whether on interior and exterior surfaces, coatings should also be able to withstand all types of abuse, and most importantly...

He paused, pulling out a flat sample of a product that had a proven track record being used all over the world. It was from the only company he ever used. Otis held it up for everyone to see. It was a simple, clear film, no larger than four-by-two inches, with a picture of a globe in its center.

They should be flexible. And even more crucial is that they should have elongation and be able to move with a substrate.

He stretched the flat sample and said while pulling at the film,

Every substrate or surface moves whether through expansion and contraction from heat and cold or from vibrations or normal building settling and movement." He stated that the old, oil-based coatings that were used in the past dried hard and could take a lot of abuse; however, they had little or no elongation, and when the substrates with these coatings moved, which they all do, these old coatings cracked.

The integrity of the system becomes lost. Moisture can then get under and behind the coating system and cause it to bubble and delaminate, bringing with this the problems of mold and mildew. Without elongation, the quality of a system's longevity is seriously compromised." In the time he spent talking about elongation, he continued to slowly stretch the flat sample and by the time he had finished, the globe film was now eight inches long, showing a 4000 percent elongation. After he released it, it slowly began to return to its original, size showing that it had memory.

They especially need to have a Class A fire rating, showing that they do not support combustion, and that if they do get in a fire, nothing toxic should be released. They should have extensive testing and approvals that establish their superior qualities and the testing should be performed solely by third party, independent, accredited laboratories.

Quality coatings should also be easily applied by conventional methods, such as with a brush, roller, and the less labor intensive common industry method of spraying, also known as 'Blow and Go.' Coatings should be able to be sprayed, applied, and used over difficult situations, such as uneven surfaces with peaks and valleys, like asbestos-containing spray-on fireproofing, which was generally used for fire protection of structural steel. Whether it was the hard cementious material or the light fluffy cotton candy types, the latter could release more harmful fiber when brushed or rolled. Asbestos comes in all different forms, some of which can only be sprayed on, which is the safest and fastest way to handle it. Hence, the term 'Blow and Go' spraying refers to a practice that minimizes a building's down time and the cost of relocation fees, in most cases.

Cha-Ching.

Next, Otis juggled a coated white covered glass bottle in his hand and said,

They should be able to take a lot of wear and tear and all-out abuse.

He startled the room by throwing the bottle up in the air and letting it hit the floor, only to pick it up, put it on the table, and smash it with a hammer. Most in the room pulled back instinctively as they heard the breaking glass, only to lean forward as the coated glass bottle retained its shape and the shattered glass had not showered the floor.

> This is a perfect example of what industrial protective green coatings should do.

He continued to handle the bottle, but this time, he shook and squeezed it, which caused many to flinch. The pieces of glass within the coatings resembled, in sound, a pair of Maracas.

> Here we have a hazardous material, broken glass, safely sealed inside. I can hold and even squeeze it in my hand.

———

This was the number one demonstration piece that Otis had used for years. He would explain green renewable, sustainable coatings and their requirement to be impact and abuse resistant, as well as their need to have extreme elongation. He would notice that his audience was not getting it. It seemed to go right over their heads. However, when he would take out the bottle and whack it with the hammer, everyone seemed to instantly understand what he was talking about.

He went on,

Quality matters, especially when dealing with the logical solution of in-place management of potentially hazardous materials. Quality is always less expensive in the long run. If it lasts longer, it will save you the replacement cost of materials, as well as expensive labor.

Cha-Ching.

It's the same thing with a gasoline tank or the coating over our electric cords: quality matters. We want quality, and it should be the same for the in-place management of asbestos and lead-based paint. In addition, quality coatings should be able to seal in hazards, while at the same time be sustainable and renewable. They should also accommodate building renovations and retrofitting, for example, bringing a building up to fire code with the installation of a sprinkler system (once again man handling the broken bottle with a firm squeeze.) Then the coated substrate can be clamped onto or anchored with mechanical fasteners or even drilled through with shrouded drills and saws fed into a vacuum with a HEPA (High Efficiency Particulate Air) filter, which can remove at least 99.97 percent of airborne particles.

Labor is the largest cost on most projects, so if time and expense are going to be invested in a project, they should not be wasted on coatings that will fail after a short period of time. Planned obsolescence should not even be considered when it comes to hazardous materials, or on any project, as far as I'm concerned.

One of the largest potential areas of concern to the health of the general public, all over the world, is asbestos exposure from roofing, which is still being manufactured and used. In-place management, using green, renewable, and sustainable coatings, is the simplest and most environmentally advanced way of dealing with it, especially if those coatings have all the characteristics and approvals for containing asbestos while at the same time waterproofing and possessing all the features for a solar/heat reflective, renewable roof system. There should never be a reason to have to do a roof tear off, causing the transportation disposal and storage in a land fill, triggering roof replacement, as with a lot of the past and current roof systems. Roofs should be seamless, continuous, and monolithic. Seams on roofs are predominantly where you encounter the most problems with water penetration. Wind infiltration can also get beneath and rip them off, especially in times of high winds during hurricanes, typhoons, and tornadoes.

Roofs also must be solar/heat reflective to repel the suns rays and not draw heat in, thus reducing cooling loads and saving energy. Roofs coated with white reflective coatings normally stay 50 to 60 degrees cooler at peak times than traditional, darker roofing. These reflective or Cool Roof systems are one of the best methods for keeping solar heat out while increasing energy savings. They preserve the environment, saving money by keeping the building cooler, thus reducing electrical demands and time by reducing cooling system wear and tear, meaning reduced downtime and maintenance expense. NASA has done studies that show installing a white solar/heat reflective roofing system gives a one-year return on your investment.

Everything erodes over time, and it's a well known and practical fact that it is far better to have a sacrificial renewable green coating wear away over time then the actual substrate it's protecting. The sacrificial coating should be renewable, meaning that even after say, twenty years, you should be able to recoat over the old coating and have it cross-link bond with the existing one, so they can't be separated and the old and new become one composite system, avoiding tear off, disposal, and replacement. This type of renewable system can save a lot of TEM, such as with landfills that are more and more in short supply.

Another important point that Otis brought up was case by case System Designs.

Every situation, whether you're dealing with asbestos, lead-based paint, weatherproofing, roofing, or other environmental issues are all different as most things in life are. One solution will not solve every challenge. One size doesn't fit all. Systems should always be designed around the clients' needs and what the project requires to obtain the desired outcome. Sometimes primers are needed and other times not. Spread factors, along with wet and dry thickness amounts, will vary depending on the surfaces they are being used to protect, as with interior or exterior, roofing or walls, and how long they need to hold up—hence, case by case.

Even if a building is to be demolished, say in five years, it's still easier to maintain the hazardous materials in-place and deal with them when the building is unoccupied, at the end of its life cycle. Also, if the hazardous materials in question are sealed in-place, they are easier to handle and can be disposed of in large chunks, as opposed to scraping and bagging all these materials separately. In some of our older, larger cities, some of these buildings were constructed at the end of the last century and are still in great shape, and if the outsides of these buildings are maintained, there is no telling how long they may last.

In his early years of in place management, both Chief and Otis had been involved with a fiasco where an asbestos coating was used in the wrong way, and instead of solving the problem, it had only added to it, creating the impression that in-place management did not work. In fact, in most cases, the issue not only concerns the system design, method of application, and type of product but how they are all implemented together.

At the time, Chief was just starting to understand the benefits of leaving asbestos alone and putting a coating over it to stop exposure. It was explained to him that in-place management was a great way to go, and so he gave his approval on a project. Unfortunately, the project designer who had made the recommendation didn't know the vast difference between coating materials, system design, and what their intended uses were. As a result, a post-removal water-thin coating was used and failed, instead of using a tough, green coating, made of industrial protective material, which acted as a flexible, abuse-resistant membrane over the asbestos.

Otis concluded with,

We've had people, all day today, talking about how potentially dangerous these hazards are, and this is true. I do believe it was dead-wrong to push the panic button on asbestos and lead-based paint, calling for the full removal, transportation, disposal, storage, and replacement of these building materials.

Asbestos and lead-based paint should be managed in-place, just like electricity, gas, gasoline, or water. A law to have it all removed would be like calling for the removal of water from our lives because some people have drowned, or removing electricity because people have been electrocuted. Better to safely manage all of them.

He quoted Donald Trump, one of the most savvy real-estate developers in the world, who stated in his third book that asbestos had gotten a 'bad rap' and that "it is the greatest fireproofing material ever used, and everybody in the construction industry knows it." Truer words have never been spoken.

Otis had just single handedly hit a game winning homerun, with Marcos and Lyn to follow with some icing and a cherry for the cake.

Marcos the Smooth began. True to his appearance, Marcos spoke with a deep voice, tonal-rich in knowledge and confirmation. He knew what he was talking about, and those who listened felt it.

Let's start by breaking the challenges of these materials down with six questions, also known as Kipling's Six Serving Men.

- Who is affected by the hazardous exposure of asbestos and lead-based paint? That is all of us, worldwide, directly and indirectly. You've heard all the studies and the research spoken about today, and like the greenhouse effect of global warming, climate change, and pollution, there is no where to run from it. These problems affect all of us. We all live downstream. Who is responsible? We all are. We all need to be proactive in preventing unnecessary removal and exposure of these hazardous materials.

- What are the undeniable and easily prevented health effects that can come from unnecessary exposure to these hazards.

- <u>Where</u> are these hazards? Everywhere. Worldwide. We are all living downstream. Where are the solutions? Everywhere! In our homes, work places, schools, and our environment. Both asbestos and lead-based paint have been around since ancient times. Asbestos has been heavily used since the industrial revolution, in all types of building materials, everything from roofing systems to floor tiles. As for lead-based paint, they were extensively used, and even though they were known hazards, they were at times even endorsed by federal governments.

- <u>When</u> should we take action? Now! When most people hear about the potential dangers of asbestos and lead-based paint we tend to do nothing. When we need to take practical action rather than to go to the extremes of removing it all or recommending full removal instead of management in-place, I ask why? Because we feel that it doesn't affect us. We tend to think it only affects the poor or that it could never happen to us. It's not until we realize that it's affecting all of us, that we want to do something.

- <u>Why</u> did we use them? Because they were the best materials available, and we weren't as aware of the downside.

- <u>How</u> can we manage these hazardous materials, and how can we stop unnecessary exposure? When dealing with hazards like asbestos and lead-based paint, at the moment, the laws states that it must be first identified and then abated. It doesn't say that we must remove them. Why? Because it would not be economically, environmentally, or logically possible. In short, it can't be done. There isn't enough money in the world to remove all these hazards. Also, it doesn't make any sense. It would be like saying we need to remove fire and water because people get burned and drown. In addition, there isn't enough space to properly store these hazards, and hopefully, there aren't enough people silly enough to try. The proper removal of asbestos and lead-based paint is very costly in TEM, and to do nothing is not an option."

Next Marcos went on to the balance sheet.

Let's now look at how removal and management in-place compare and contrast." He had prepared a balance sheet that had been handed out.

Methods of abatement can be accomplished via coatings; hard barriers, like sheet rock, contact or wall paper, duct tape, trowel applied materials, plaster, concrete, etc; and finally, removal and replacement. While there are numerous abatement methods, the two methods we're going to focus on in this balance sheet are coatings and removal.

In viewing this balance sheet we are going to look at TEM. Time is an uncontrollable event that lacks bias and waits for no one. Next on the list is the environment; we're going to look at the environmental effects. By environment, I refer to the environment in which we live, our health, and our future. Lastly, I will look at money, the aspect that tends to be the deciding factor when dealing with issues of health and hazardous concerns."

PROJECT FACTORS	IN-PLACE MANAGEMENT	REMOVAL & REPLACEMENT
METHODS	Encase with conventionally applied, preferably green coatings.	The removal of the hazardous materials and replacement.
JOBSITE PREPARATION STAGES	Overspray or splatter protection with plastic or drop cloths.	Full containment with layers of plastic covering all the surfaces that will not be removed. Negative air machines to provide a clean air exchange every 15 minutes. Decontamination chambers with a dirty room to remove all contaminated clothes, a shower room to wash yourself and your respirator. A clean room to dress in your street clothes.
LABOR FORCE	Knowledge of how to use a paint brush, roller, or conventional airless sprayer.	Trained, medically tested, hazardous material certified, respirator fit tested and licensed removal workers. Skilled laborers to replace the removed material.
EQUIPMENT	Brush, roller or conventional airless sprayer.	Full or half face respirators, sometimes with outside supplied air. Disposable suits, air monitoring pumps, negative air machines, scrapers, duct tape, special bags, brushes, rollers, sprayers and decontamination chambers.
JOBSITE PROCEDURES	Apply the green coatings with brush, roller or conventional airless sprayer	First set up full containment then wet scrape and bag all the removed material. Follow with a lock down of any remaining fibers. Do air monitoring before breaking down containment and replace the removed materials.
AFTER PROCEDURE	Let Dry.	Apply coating to lock down any of the remaining hazard that is not visible to the naked eye. Replace the removed hazard with a product of equal or greater value.
CLEAN UP	Water rinse of equipment.	Special bagging of the hazardous materials and removal and bagging of the first layer of plastic before air monitoring clearance samples.
TRANSPORTATION OF WASTE	None	Special trucks to transport the hazardous waste.
DISPOSAL	None	Special hazardous materials location.
STORAGE	None	Special hazardous materials storage location with lifetime ownership.
LOCATION DOWNTIME	Depending on size: 0 to 24 Hours. Most often same day turnaround.	Considerable downtime - depending upon project size and scope of work.
ENVIRONMENTAL FACTORS	Any coatings used should have low VOCs, and no ozone depleting substances. They should also be "Green" and environmentally advanced, solar reflective, and with little or no impact on the environment.	The removal process increases the chance of exposure, loss of environmental area for storage and the removed materials do not easily break down, lasting for generations. Also studies show that 42% of CO_2 emissions causing greenhouse gases are coming from overflowing landfills.
RELOCATION FEES	In most cases none.	The costs are considerably extensive. Studies show that for every dollar spent on a direct cost, there is another dollar spent on indirect cost such as with building downtime, people and office relocation.

After going over the balance sheet, Marcos brought out his other handouts, some pie charts and graphs, showing how much of the materials in question were present not just nationwide but also globally.

All of his information pointed to the massive amounts of these materials present and the overwhelming expense it would take to remove and replace them.

The handouts also clearly showed the many benefits of management in-place, not just stopping the release of potentially hazardous materials. As in the case of asbestos-containing roofing, you are sealing in the asbestos and at the same time waterproofing the roof while making it solar/heat reflective adding tremendous energy savings. There was an added benefit to using this type of system on roofs that were made out of coal, tar-based, asphalt materials, showing ground water contamination from rain runoff that is instantly stopped as soon as the roof is coated. This of course can only be accomplished by choosing the right coating materials. The best part is that the original material is left in place doing what it was intended to do.

Marcos concluded,

> We've all been taught that knowledge is power, but the truth is that "knowledge plus action is power." Marcus held up the balance sheet, "here is the knowledge. Management in-place is the obvious and best practical action. You have the knowledge; now what are you going to do with it?"

> Lyn the Sensitive, AKA Ms. Caring started by saying,

> I know that it has been a long day for everyone and that for many of you, there has been a lot of new information presented, while for others, previously known information was reconfirmed or disproved. So I won't reiterate the information presented throughout today, but instead, I'll provide closure on much of the information and place the logical decision in your more than capable hands.

While I haven't been present for the bulk of today's panels, I was able to read the information that would be presented today, and I must admit that the idea of 'remove it or leave it alone' falls short of logic but ranks high in expense, both human and monetary.

In a gentle but clear voice she said,

The myopic thinking behind 'remove it or leave it alone' is attributed to the same ideology that produced the unnecessary asbestos panic and prolonged the use of lead-based paint. If we want to improve, to do better for our loved ones, the general population, and for the future of the planet, we must think globally while acting locally.

In this age of global warming, climate change, escalating oil prices, food shortages, and diminishing natural resources, we urgently have to think more about going green while we recycle as much as we possibly can, which at the top of the list includes our buildings. By doing this we can minimize what we dispose of in our shrinking landfills, help reduce CO_2 emissions, and use the funds for more humanitarian and planetary needs.

Lyn had stated many times that a lot of the issues that were brought up today should be included in the Office of Homeland Security, especially the exposure from lead-based paint and its adverse affect on certain groups of the population.

We can all agree it's not possible to remove all the asbestos and lead-based paint which was and is used all over the world. For example, starting with our schools and all the problems plaguing our education system, the budgetary concerns and limited funds could be freed up from unneeded asbestos and lead-based paint removal projects. As stated previously, one school spent over a million dollars to have asbestos removed transported, stored, and replaced. How can we propose the same to schools that lack fundamental tools such as chairs, desks, and textbooks, and where the teachers are overworked and underpaid?

Simple in-place management solutions shouldn't just be considered for schools; it should be as mandatory as teachers, classrooms and books. We put the asbestos in our schools for a reason; let it do its job.

The reality of asbestosis, lung cancer, mesothelioma, and other asbestos-induced diseases, as well as lead-based paint exposure, are a danger to us all. Each year, more and more victims are unnecessarily subjected to asbestos and lead-based paint exposure here in the U.S. and around the world, if only because of a lack of education on how simple the solutions really are.

Looking around the room, she continued,

I have personally experienced the loss of a loved one to the effects of asbestosis. Twenty-seven years ago, my husband was taken from me, so when I speak of these issues, I speak from the heart. In-place management is a logical method of abatement, and I do not speak for it lightly. I don't blame the utilization of this useful material, only the ignorance on how to handle it. Asbestos and lead-based paint need to be properly controlled, and this should be done by managing it in-place, and the simplest way to do that is with green, protective coatings.

When it comes to asbestos exposure and lead poisoning, we are all susceptible. It is our children, however, who are the hapless victims that will sustain lifelong mental and physical damage. The ingestion of lead via lead sources such as lead-based paint chips and lead dust has been linked to cognitive decline in children's language development, processing speed, eye-hand coordination, executive functioning, motor skills, verbal memory and learning, visual memory, and reduced IQ scores. This in turn frustrates the individual, often leading to disciplinary challenges and anti social behavior, potentially leading a path toward prison. This is all because of a lack of understanding and identification of the damage being done and how it can be prevented.

Also, the earliest studies show that exposure to lead, from before birth into adulthood, can permanently damage the brain. It is connected to increased criminal behavior, leading to large arrest numbers, particularly for violent crime. This is a statistically disturbing and significant correlation between elevated concentrations of lead in the blood throughout prenatal and postnatal stages of development and higher criminal arrest rates during adulthood.

These aggressive, hostile, or violent behavioral activities often emerge early and continue throughout life.

Lead exposure during childhood amplifies the potential of being incarcerated for violent crime. It is also associated with volume loss in areas of the brain connected with problem solving and judgment.

Researchers found that after age eighteen, individuals with increased blood-lead levels during prenatal stages and early childhood exhibited higher rates of arrest for violent crimes than the rest of the population.

A public health priority should be identifying the risk factors that may place youth on an early path toward a life of crime and violence, taking solid, economical practical steps to prevent it.

Studies also strongly report increased lead exposure leading to increased blood-lead levels also correlated with higher rates of arrest for nonviolent as well as violent crimes. Childhood lead exposure is now an acknowledged risk factor for aggressive, antisocial behavior, attention deficit hyperactivity disorder and juvenile delinquency.

Chief couldn't help but sympathetically wonder if this may have been one of the contributing factors to Dracoff's misguided life leading him down a dishonorable path as Lyn continued,

Lower income, inner-city children remain particularly vulnerable to lead exposure, due to the poor quality and maintenance of their housing. We've made great strides in reducing lead exposure, and findings send a clear message that further reduction of childhood lead exposure is an important and simple necessity. The fact that studies are able to detect and follow the effects from childhood exposures into adulthood stands as a testament to lead's power to influence behavior over a long period of time.

There is a strong argument that the lead in bullets is not the only lead that causes the overflowing of prisons, but the effects from lead-based paint exposure, stimulating the wrong decisions and antisocial behavior are also contributing to filling our prisons.

The question we need to ask ourselves is who is more criminal: the individuals who are unknowingly exposed to breaking down lead-based paint or the ones who are aware of the harmful effects and can do something about it but don't.

Originally 10 ug/dl was established as the 'safe' blood lead level, but in 1991, the Centers for Disease Control and Prevention (CDCP) declared that 10 ug/dl was in fact unsafe. That blood lead level number was originally established because it was the lowest blood lead level that could be detected with inexpensive testing. It was not because it was the level at which symptoms of poisoning appeared. The CDCP reasoning for this was that setting the standard any lower would only burden the country's health-care system even though symptoms of lead poisoning were observed in children and lab monkeys at blood lead levels of 5 ug/dl and lower, half of the CDCP currently established safe level. In reality, there is no safe exposure limit, and why would anyone knowingly expose people, especially our children, to any hazard that could be easily prevented?

We found out that asbestos and lead-based paint only had to be abated, not removed and replaced, like information we had heard from previous sources.

Chief thought that now the lead-based paint facts, research, and issues were on the front burner and that research had shown there was not enough money in the world to remove it all. Everything pointed to in-place management; what works for lead also works for asbestos. People started to logically ask if we can in-place manage most lead-based paint, why can't it work for asbestos. People were catching on, and this pleased Chief.

On top of this was the evidence from the scientific community that at least 40% of the CO2 emissions causing green house gases and largely contributing to global warming/climate change were coming from landfills. These landfills were being unnecessarily filled up with the unwanted waste generated from the early removal and demolition of buildings.

There are currently claims of economic and ethnic inequity concerning lead poisoning. It was in 1952 when the first signs of socioeconomic and racial discrimination associated with lead poisoning were discovered in the City of Baltimore. The head of the Baltimore health department wrote that children of African-American descent had 7.5 times the blood lead level of their Caucasian-American counterparts. At the time of the testing, only 30 percent of the pre-school population tested was African-American, leading to the thought that environmental factors due to economic disadvantage were to blame for the disproportionate poisoning.

At present, the situation has changed little. According to the CDCP's 1998 study, African-American children still show the highest concentrations of lead in children ages one to five. Of those living in homes and apartments built before 1946, 21.9 percent of them have blood lead levels of 10 ug/dl or more. Those living in homes and apartments built between 1946 and 1973 also have blood lead levels of 10 ug/dl and higher.

A study of children who live in Philadelphia's inner city and have visited pediatric clinics showed that 68 percent of them had blood lead levels above the 'safe' 10 ug/dl level. When you consider all the data, more than one million African-Americans and other minority children who live in our inner city areas are constantly being poisoned by lead exposure.

Extensive studies have shown that it would be a lot wiser and less expensive to proactively deal with the cause of this problem rather than just reacting to its symptoms.

In 1991, the Centers for Disease Control published a study showing that while it would cost taxpayers $32 billion to have lead abated in inner city homes, it would save taxpayers $60 billion in heath-care and special-education costs alone not to mention incarceration fees for those exposed. However, to date, this information has yet to be acted on by adopting this cost-effective course of action. Instead, generation after generation of inner city youth with diminished intellectual capacity and a penchant toward violence add to the numbers of our already over-crowded prisons.

Lyn's voice hit a high pitch as she emphasized,

Along with the disproportionate exposure to hazardous materials there is also bias to people of color present in the educational and justice systems compounding the problems.

So far, the canary in the coal mine approach of testing children to find out if a home, housing complex, or building is exposing children to lead is nothing short of backwards, if not grossly negligent.

The idea of children being used to test lead the same way canaries were used to test for gases in coal mines sent a vivid image around the room. The Chief thought of his own child, when she was small, and now his grandchildren. He loved them so much and would do anything for them, even gladly laying down his life for them.

Chief wasn't easily disturbed. He could and would sometimes over look ignorance, and yet, he fumed over deliberate child neglect and mistreatment. Even as a youth, if something bothered him, he had a quiet calmness about himself, evaluating even the most emotional situations and deciding the best course of action to take. At the time when he found out that children were being used as lead testers, as Lyn said, comparing them to canaries in a coal mine, all of that was put to the test. He was furious when he found out that innocent children were knowingly being lead poisoned and that actions were not being taken to save the children, but to save money. How shameless!

Looking around the room at the surprised, sympathetic faces of those who heard this for the first time, he could only imagine the pain and suffering of the parents who found out their child had been unnecessarily poisoned by the often deliberate exposure to lead-based paint. It was shocking to many discovering that this disease was not genetic, hereditary, or some unfortunate accident; but that it was easily preventable, that its damaging effects are irreversible, and that it was nothing short of careless disregard on the part of certain decision makers to save money over lives. He couldn't stand the thought that even one child was being poisoned who could be protected, but this is why they were there, because children and adults alike were being unnecessarily poisoned.

Chief looked over at Dracoff, and surprisingly, he saw what looked like a glimmer of understanding for the hapless victims, if not a downright hint of sorrow and sympathy, possibly for the unfortunate little ones.

Lyn continued,

> If a home or building was built before 1974 it should be assumed it has some asbestos or lead-based paint and be dealt with as such to make sure the occupants are not unnecessarily exposed. As my co-panelist explained previously, it has been proven that trying to remove lead-based paint actually increases the risk of lead exposure, via fumes and dust. If the proper precautions are not taken, large amounts of lead could be breathed in or deposited elsewhere in a home where it could later be ingested.

This was another example of why Chief felt so strongly about getting the word out and making sure everyone understood all of the aspects of removal and replacement. It was not only a last resort, but the more expensive and unnecessary recourse.

The safer, cost effective, most logical approach would be to cover up and in-place manage these potential hazardous with a quality, green, sustainable, and renewable coating system. When it comes to our loved ones safety, we should all plan for the best.

We are our children's future, and our children are our future. It is what we give them that we will reap when we are older. We don't have all the solutions of how to deal with the poison and hazards that were created and handed down to us, but our children should have the best chance to take a crack at them. If we can't solve the problem, we should at least minimize and abate it. We must lessen the chances of these potentially hazardous materials from prematurely crippling our youth before they can answer its call.

Is in-place management with green coatings perfect? Yes, for this situation it is. The overall best method of using and living with these potential hazards is far better than doing nothing. Coating over them is the most practical solution. The cost of doing nothing is much too high a price compared with taking logical action.

In closing, asbestos and lead-based paint are very serious issues that threaten our loved ones, homes, and environment. They're an environmental time bomb that can't be ignored by hoping they go away. And yet, there is a very simple solution. In theory, the removal of these hazards may sound well-grounded, but there's not enough money in the world to remove them all. The only ecological, economical, and realistic way of immediately handling these hazards is to manage them in-place with industrial, protective, green coatings.

As Lyn finished, Chief looked over at the deflated Dracoff knowing he had over played his loathsome hand. Everyone present knew that unless there was a building demolition or a remodel requiring removal and disposal, Chief's case for in-place management of asbestos and lead-based paint with affordable, green coatings was the best.

Ironically, Dracoff had never believed that his deliberate disregard for the health problems associated with these hazardous materials would cause him any trouble, other than the potential loss of money. In fact, they may have been contributing factors in the misguided life he had led so far.

In the end, years later, Dracoff suffered a slow and torturous death, caused by his long term exposure to these materials, which were ever-present and consistently ignored on his jobsites and in the buildings he owned and lived in. The very buildings that brought him huge ill-gotten gains ended up contributing to his demise.

It was getting late, and it had been a long day filled with lots of information and plenty of emotion. Now, as everyone filtered out of the room, Chief stayed to give his final instructions to his staff, making sure that the video, audio, and transcripts of the day would be duplicated and sent to all the interested parties. In the days to come, the internet blogs on the day's proceedings would be in the thousands.

CHAPTER 12

Chief's Crusade

Chief sat in the quiet calm of the aftermath in the testimony chamber. The snow had stopped piling up outside, and even though the windows were still open, all the snow was absorbing sound, adding to the reflective hush of the chamber. Only a half hour earlier, the room had been jammed packed, standing room only, filled with inquiring minds. He contemplated his next move.

He was supposed to move to Florida and live with his daughter and her family. He loved his daughter, and yet he knew he'd be bored stiff. Lyn had just made him an offer that would be hard to refuse. She was booked for the next six months traveling around the world giving talks on the effects of lead-based paint and asbestos exposure and what preventable action that could be taken to limit those effects. With a twinkle in her eye, she made an invitation for him to come along with her, presenting the findings on in-place management. He had kept in touch with Lyn over the years with phone calls and e-mails, yet it was a good five years since he had last seen her in person. When she came through the doors earlier that day, his heartbeat jumped, reconfirming his feelings for her.

What should he do? It would not be a tough choice: traveling and living with The Beautiful Ms. Lyn or atrophying in Florida. He had to laugh and ask himself if that was a trick question: to wither or not? He didn't need a Ben Franklin balance sheet or Kipling's Six Serving Men to answer this one. When Lyn asked him, he almost had to pinch himself to see if he was awake.

He was definitely taking Lyn up on her offer and was formulating a plan to incorporate her schedule with his, in order to get the word out on the advantages of in-place management. He'd start by reaching out to all the contacts worldwide that he'd developed over the years, getting meetings set up in all the places they would be traveling to, getting in front of as many high-ranking decision makers as possible. Then he would set up appointments for as many talk radio and television shows he could get on. It didn't matter if they were in some small town in the middle of the night or on Oprah, as long as they were willing to listen, he'd be willing to talk and answer questions.

He felt super excited and extremely relieved, knowing that his life would continue to have a useful purpose helping others. He'd woke up this morning heading into retirement, feeling somewhat saddened and discontented knowing it was the last day at his job, ending his long career of serving others. Now, just hours later, he was rejuvenated with the thought of committing to go on the road with Lyn. It also confirmed his belief that one day and one person can make a world of positive difference in the lives of many. Lyn had done just that for him, which would in turn trickle down to all the lives he would continue to help. It also confirmed that for every door that closes, another one opens.

Great things were also happening with Otis and Marcos. They had started a foundation, with each contributing a million dollars. They had many affluent friends and contacts, all of whom had already agreed to contribute numerous funds. The foundation would help needy landlords and governments all over the world that were supplying low income housing for the less fortunate.

They would do an Encasement Makeover to buildings, using green coatings for the in-place management of hazardous materials, as well as waterproofing while turning walls and roofing solar/heat reflective, saving energy. They would turn decrepit buildings that were slated for demolition into green, energy efficient, affordable housing.

As it turned out one of the first ones on the list to help was the landlord who testified on Dracoff's panel. They found out that he really was a decent guy who was housing many needy people, never tossing out anyone who couldn't come up with their rent, and almost never making a profit.

And so it went, with everything being righteous and just at the end of the day.

Whoosh.

———

Made in the USA
Lexington, KY
31 October 2012